Broken Walls and a Hospital Gown

Paula Macena

Broken Walls and a Hospital Gown

ISBN: 9780692471432

CHAPTER ONE

Bookworm.

That is what I am. I'm that person who doesn't worry about life because I'm too busy worrying about a fictional character's. In the entire fifteen years that I have lived on this planet, never have I found anyone that is just like me. I mean, I have one best friend, but we're complete opposites. That's why we're friends, I guess. We push each other to new experiences.

I read every single day of my life. I can't go a day without it. But since I'm in high school, I have to start taking "responsibility" and start "thinking about my future."

Believe me, I've tried. And since they say being a dragon isn't an option, I got nothing. School is supposed to help, and I guess sometimes it does. Even if some of the teachers are rude and lazy, and half of my friends-that-are-now-ex-friends turned out to be fake, and I can never remember my locker combination, and I sit alone at lunch, and the highest grade I've gotten in my life was an A- (and that was back in elementary school), and I'm 99.9% sure that the principal has a time-warping machine in her office to make school last longer ... yeah. Sometimes it helps.

Everyone there hates me. I honestly don't know why. I have never done anything to them. If you keep your nose in a book, or get good grades, or mess up just once, they all turn on you, even if it doesn't concern them.

There are also some other things that lead up to one big thing. Let's see if you can guess it:

A small paper cut can bleed for days.

I am very pale.

I go running or walking very often, but I have to be careful not to pass out.

I get insomnia.

My lips are also very pale.

I'm cold in the summer.

I'm very thin.

By choice.

All this equals one thing:

I am anorexic.

Or at least that's what they call it.

"Marissa Anne?" the teacher calls. I lift my head in confusion. *Me*?

There's a reason why I sit in the back of the class. *To not get called on.* Why don't teachers ever call on people who are actually raising their hand?

"Marissa?" the teacher calls again. "Do you know the answer?" I look at the problem she's indicating on the board. What is this? What kind of cruel, evil mind created math? Gosh, isn't addition enough? Why do we even have math? It's not like I'm actually going to need it in the future, no matter how much they say I will. That is one of the biggest lies of my childhood. No, I mean *of my life.* I will never, ever need this. Every person in the world knows how to count, and I just don't feel like multiplying or using exponents or fractions. Or Pi. Why in the world is Pi so important? It's just some long decimal!

"Marissa!" the teacher practically yells. "The answer?" People are snickering now. I roll my eyes at them, and shrug at the teacher. "Should've known," she mutters.

I turn back to my notebook, pretending to take notes when I'm doing anything *but* that. Drawing, writing, whatever. They already told me I'm passing.

That's good enough for me.

I draw a picture of my teacher, her mouth open, pointing at an evil problem on the board, hoping to make us fail. The bell finally rings, and I grab my stuff and leave as quickly as I can.

"Marissa?" Not fast enough. I turn around, expecting some big long speech about how important it is to pay attention in class, and then a note home to my mom that I'll probably throw away. Instead, it's much worse. "I'm getting you a tutor," the teacher says.

"Sorry?" I say, thinking, hoping, praying that I had misunderstood.

"A tutor," she repeats. "You obviously have trouble understanding, or even paying attention at all. You could use the extra help."

"But I'm passing," I say.

"For now," she says. "But school only started a few weeks ago. I wouldn't take chances if I were you." *But I'm* not *you,* I think to myself. "Either way, you don't have much of a choice," she says, reading my mind. "Go to the library after school, and he'll meet you there."

He? I think as she writes up a note. *Great, this day just keeps getting better and better.* I take the note and walk out of the classroom. I look at my phone to check the time. I'm going to be late for my next class. Marvelous. I get to my locker and put in my combination. *Not working.*

I try again. *Still not working.*

Again. *Crud.*

I groan and punch the locker in frustration.

"Bad day, huh?" a voice says.

"Back off," I say without turning around.

"You'll be fine," the voice says. "The day is almost over anyway."

"I said, back off," I reply, this time turning to my left to see who's talking. A boy. He seems familiar.

"Okay," he says, surrendering. "Just trying to cheer you up."

"Why cheer up someone you don't even know?"

He shrugs. "I like seeing people smile. It's nice, you know? Especially when you're the one who put that smile there." I turn back to my locker and try to put the combination in again. *Denied.* "You'll get it eventually," the boy says. "It can't keep you locked out forever." I sigh. He's relentless.

I try again. This time I hear a little click, and my locker pops open. "See?" he says, smiling and gives a little wave. "See you around." When he's not looking, I allow myself to give a small smile. He's strange.

Good.

I'm not the only one.

It's four o'clock. I'm waiting in the library for whoever my tutor is, but I seem to be the only one there. *Maybe the teacher got the time wrong,* I think. *Or maybe the tutor decided not to show up.*

I look around at the library, full of books that people don't bother to read anymore, mostly textbooks. *I don't blame him.*

I stand up from the desk I'm sitting at and start to walk around. I've never really bothered to come to this library, no matter how much I love books. From what I've heard, it's full of textbooks, and I couldn't care less for those.

I go down the aisles, looking for something worth reading, something that teaches me something that's not math, or science or social studies, or anything that they could teach you in a public high school.

Nothing.

I am about to enter the next aisle when a sound catches my attention. Someone whistling. A sweet, catchy tune. I look around to find where the music is coming from but stay in the shadows the shelves cast.

I walk up and down the aisles until I reach the one that is marked *Poetry*.

The music is coming from there. I peek around the corner to see someone standing there, looking at books of Shakespeare and Emily Dickinson. He looks about my age, but I don't think I've seen him before.

The way he looks and stands seems to say *outcast,* but he doesn't seem to mind the label. He glances my way, and I hide, hoping he doesn't see me. When I glance back, again he is gone. *What ...?*

"Hi." I gasp, and quickly turn to my right. It's him. *How did he get here so fast?*

"Are you Marissa Anne?" he asks, and I nod. He extends his hand. "Nice to meet you. I'm Graham Welf." I glance at his hand, and then look back at him. Once he realizes I'm not going to take it, he awkwardly lowers it to his side. "Um, I'm your tutor," he says. I thought he'd be older, like a college guy, but he seems to be my age. I think about saying something but instead stare at the floor.

"Look, you're going to have to talk at some point," he says, exasperated already. "So you might as well start."

"I'm not the talkative type," I say quietly.

"Well, you need to start *being* the talkative type," he replies. "At least to me. Or else the rest of the school year and maybe even next year is going to be awkward for the both of us. Okay?"

"Fine," I say. "Why are you so pushy?"

"I'm only pushy when I need to be," he says. "Now let's just sit down, and start working."

"Okay." We walk over to the desk and put our books down in front of us.

"What are you having trouble with?" he asks.

I shrug.

He face palms.

"We are going to get nowhere if you don't start saying something. Anything," he says.

"I already have."

"You need to say more."

"Why?"

"Why *not?*"

"I just don't want to, okay?"

He sighs. "Please, the least you can do is make an effort. I want to help."

"Do you want to, or do you *have* to?" I ask.

"I *want* to," he says. "Literally, I volunteered for this. I am not playing you."

Now I'm curious. "Why would you volunteer for this?"

He shrugs. "I just wanted to, okay?"

Even though I don't want to, I smile. I can't help it. "Fine. Let's start working." As we work, I take glances at him and put the pieces of his face together in my mind. His big brown eyes, his straight black hair, the dimple in his left cheek, and the smirk he does when he knows he's right.

Who is he? He seems sincere, but how can I be sure? And why would he volunteer to help? All in all, it wasn't so bad. He actually helps me understand more.

"Meet me here tomorrow?" he says.

"Do I have a choice?" I reply, and then we go our separate ways. Different.

Maybe there are people like me out there, after all.

I've missed the bus, so I have to walk home. It's about three miles away, so thankfully, it's not much. *Gosh, I can't wait to get home and sleep. And read. And, of course, go online.*

I walk down different streets on the way home, looking at houses and people, and I wonder what they're going through, what their life is like, and what they see and hear and feel. Do I know any of them? Does any of them know *me?*

I pass by a house where a guy sits on the front porch, talking to someone. I look away and keep walking. Who is that, anyway?

I can't help myself, and I look back again. This time, he's not talking to his friend. He's staring at *me.* I study him and notice how familiar he looks. Where have I seen him before? School? The park? The corner store? It could be anywhere, really.

It's weird. I should've been able to recognize a face like that, one that's so easy to remember, with that light brown hair and his hazel eyes.

His eyes are beautiful.

He smiles at me, a big cheeky smile, and I give him a half smile back. I look away, but I can tell he doesn't, and he's not even embarrassed. He won't turn his head as if he might miss something, some small detail if he looks away for just one second, so he doesn't, and I can feel his eyes on me until I turn the corner.

CHAPTER TWO

Once I get home, I simply drop my bag inside, grab my skateboard, and head in the direction of the park.

"Where are you going?" my mom asks, opening the door.

I turn around. "Just to the park."

"Be back before eight, okay?" she says.

"Okay." I wave and continue walking. Once I turn the corner, I freeze.

The same guy that was staring at me before is still sitting there, in that same spot. This time, he's alone. I guess his friend left. I shake my head, trying to focus, and then I continue walking. I'm being stupid. We don't even know each other.

"No point in having a skateboard if you're not going to use it, right?" he says.

He doesn't make it easy to ignore him.

I turn toward him. "Do I know you?"

"No," he says.

"Then mind your business, please," I snap.

"You didn't let me finish," he says. "We go to school together."

"I go to school with a lot of people," I say. "It doesn't mean I talk to them."

"Then why don't you start?"

"Why *should* I?"

"Why *shouldn't* you?" I tilt my head, trying to make sense of this guy, sitting a few feet away from me, bothering to even take notice of me, and I remember a part of the conversation I had with Graham Welf earlier today.

"Why?"

"Why not?"

The random guy smiles at my confusion. "Your name is Marissa Anne … right?"

"How do you know that?"

"I've seen you around," he says. "And I was in your class this morning when you didn't know the answer."

"Shut up."

He puts his hands up in mock surrender. "You asked, I answered."

I roll my eyes and begin to walk away.

"Wait," he says, and I stop. "I haven't introduced myself yet."

"I never asked you to."

"I want to," he says. "I'm Leon Graeme."

Then I know where I saw him.

"You were at my locker this morning."

"Yes," he says. "And you're the girl who couldn't get her locker combination."

"Why do you always point out my mistakes?"

"We just met, so I wouldn't count that as always," he says. "And a mistake is something like breaking a plate or crashing a car—unless you did that on purpose—but forgetting a locker combination is very common these days."

"You're very optimistic," I say, smiling a bit.

"You get used to it," he says.

"Well, it was nice meeting you, Leon Graeme the optimist," I say.

"It was very nice meeting you, too, Marissa Anne the curious," he says.

"Curious?" I ask.

"Of course," he says. "I can tell. You wonder a lot. Lots of people do that. Sometimes you even wonder why the sky is blue or why grass is green."

"How would you know?" I say. "I just met you."

"I can tell a lot of things about a lot of people just by the way they look, and act," he explains.

"Do you do that?" I ask. "Wonder a lot?"

His smile grows bigger, and his eyes shine. "All the time."

I smile back and walk away.

"Hey," he says, and I turn. "You gonna use that skateboard?"

I roll my eyes. "What do you think I'm going to the park for?"

"Just curious," he says with a smile as he waves goodbye.

I nod and then walk away, as he goes inside his house and closes the door.

All children, except one, grow up.

I'm re-reading my favorite book, *Peter Pan,* in the middle of the night.

Sure, I have school tomorrow.

Sure, I have to wake up early.

But that's what naps are for, right?

Nighttime is the only time that I can think clearly, so I take advantage of that and stay up as long as I like.

I check the time. It's three in the morning.

Might as well go to sleep now. I only have three hours left of sleep anyways.

I hear a ring and look at my phone.

Really? Right when I'm about to sleep, I get a text.

From my best friend, Rose.

Are you busy?

Is she kidding?

No, I'm skydiving in Europe.

She texts back immediately.

You know what I mean. Anyway, think that tomorrow we could hang out?

Where?

Mall?

Why am I not surprised that that's the first thing she suggests?

Sure. I'll see you at school.

Bye.

Bye.

I look for Rose in the cafeteria, but I don't see her. Probably eating somewhere else.

Good for her, but bad for me. I'm sitting alone today.

I look for a table in the corner of the room and sit down, with an apple and my book.

I flip open to the page that I stopped on, but then someone sits down next to me.

What in the …

"Hey."

Leon.

"Um, hi," I say. "I don't mean to be rude, but why are you sitting here?"

"Why?" he asks, looking confused. "Is someone else sitting here?"

"No, but, um …" my voice trails off as I try to figure out a good explanation. "I thought that you would be sitting with your friends."

"Well, aren't you my friend?" he asks.

"I just met you yesterday," I say.

"So?" he says. "That's how friendships start. They meet one day, start talking more the next, and one thing leads to another, and there you go, you have a friend."

"You have plenty of friends," I say. "Why would you need another one?"

"No, there is a difference between friends and acquaintances," he explains. "You see, a friend is someone who has your back, is there for you, and wants to hang out with you as much as you want to hang out with them. An acquaintance, on the other hand, is just someone you know who's polite. You don't really think about them that often."

"So, therefore, I'm an acquaintance," I say.

He shakes his head. "Nope. You're a friend. At least, to me you are. Because I've been thinking about you, and I want to hang out with you more."

"That's not a friend yet."

"*Yet,*" he says. "But it's more than an acquaintance."

"So then how many actual friends do you have?"

"One and a half," he says. "Graham, and you are the half."

"How about all of them?" I say, nodding towards a table full of people that I know he knows.

"Like I said," he says. "Acquaintances."

He looks at me and then notices that all I have is an apple and a book.

"What happened to your lunch?" he asks. "Did you already eat?"

I hold up my apple. "This is my lunch," I say.

"Wait, what?" he says. "You're not going to eat anything else?"

"Pretty much.

"Here," he gives me his fries. "Eat it."

"No, it's your food," I say, pushing it back to him. "And like I've said a bunch of times before, I just met you. For all I know, you could've poisoned it."

He laughs. "You have an overactive imagination."

"Is that a compliment?"

"Of course," he says, sounding surprised. "How can it *not* be?"

"I'm making sure, okay?"

I open my book and begin to read from where I left off. Leon moves a bit closer and reads the book over my shoulder.

"What's your name?" he asked.

"Wendy Moira Angela Darling," she replied with some satisfaction. "What is your name?"

"Peter Pan."

"Is this your first time reading that book?" Leon asks.

I look up at him. "No."

"How many times have you read it?"

"This is my fifth."

"Bookworm." He smiles.

"Shut up."

"That's a compliment."

"It is?"

"Yes."

"Well, do me a favor."

"What?"

"Stop with the compliments."

He smiles. "I can't promise anything. Well, except for one thing."

"Which is?"

"I promise that I only compliment special people."

"Good,"I say."Then you'll stop with the compliments."

"Nope."

"You *just* said you only compliment special people," I say, beginning to get frustrated with this guy.

"I know what I said," he says. "And I meant it."

"So you'll stop."

"No," he says. "Because I think you're pretty special. Yesterday, I said that you were curious. That's one of the best qualities in people, in my opinion. If you're not curious, if you never ask questions, you will never know what's real and what's not. And you're also a bookworm. That's something else that makes you special. If you're not a bookworm and just wait for the movie to come out, then you think the movie is amazing and the directors are genius. When really, all they did was completely kill the book. A bookworm compares the book to the movie and realizes every mistake and when they took something out that was *really* important."

"You done?" I ask, amused.

"Do you want me to be?" he asks.

"Kinda."

"Then yes, for now, I am," he says.

"*For now?*" I repeat.

"Yeah," he says. "Since we're going to be hanging out more often, then you can expect more compliments like those."

"*If* we're going to be hanging out more," I correct him. "And we probably won't be."

I take a bite of my apple and turn back to my book, hoping the conversation is over.

"Why not?" he asks.

I roll my eyes and look back at him. "Because I'm the bookworm with one friend. You're the guy with a bunch of them. We *don't* hang out."

"Says who?"

"High school rules."

"And who made the rules?"

"Society."

"Forget society," he says. "They make the stupidest rules and labels and trends and expect us to be okay, they expect us to be fine. I hate society. It's ridiculous, and I want to change it. I mean, we're only human—right?"

"You *are* society. So shut up, because if you really wanted to do something, you would've done it a long time ago." I take a bite of my apple and pray that that was enough to shut him up.

It's not.

"I'm a *part* of society," he says. "But I'm not the whole thing. And what if I only *now* realized what a screwed up world we live in?"

"How could you possibly have only noticed *now?*" I ask. "Our society has been a mess for a while now."

"You remember your childhood, don't you?"

"Of course."

"Then when you were a kid do you ever remember thinking that we live in a horrible world?"

I think back for a moment, and then slowly shake my head.

"Exactly," he says. "You were focusing on the beauty of everything."

"Okay, I see your point." I take another bite of my apple, and then stand up to throw the core away.

"Wait, is that *really* all you're going to eat today?" he asks.

"Yeah, so?" I say and walk over to the trashcan, and he follows.

"Doesn't that seem like too little?" He throws the rest of his food away.

"Why does it matter?"

"Why won't you answer my question?"

"No, it doesn't seem like too little," I say. "An apple and some water is enough to live off."

"Yeah, if you either have no food left or if you're on a strict diet that your doctor made you go on because you're overweight or something," he says. "And obviously, you're neither."

"How would you know?"

"First, if you didn't have any food left, I wouldn't see you at the McDonalds with Rose after school."

"Are you a stalker?"

"You're not the only one who likes McDonalds, you know!"

I sigh and walk out of the cafeteria with my book in my hand, and he still comes after me.

"Second, it's pretty damn obvious that you aren't overweight—"

"Well, that's not what they say."

"Who's 'they'?"

"People," I reply. "And if they say it, then it must be true."

"That's ridiculous!" he exclaims.

"It's the truth," I say.

"No, it's not!" he says. "It's *stupid!*"

I stop and turn to him. "Leon, why do you even care?"

"Like I said before, I'm your friend," he says. "So as your friend, I have the right to worry and care about you, okay?"

"Ugh." I continue walking to my locker, and he continues following.

"Do you eat at dinner or breakfast?"

"Yes."

"Do you eat the same amount you do at lunch?"

"I eat a small bowl of fruit in the morning and a salad at night," I say. "Why does it matter?"

"Marissa, really, this isn't healthy."

We arrive at my locker, and I put in my combination. "They have a word for it, you know," I say. "They call it anorexic."

"Does anyone else know?" he asks.

"Rose," I say. "That's about it. No one else has even cared enough to ask."

"Your parents?"

"Like you mentioned before, I eat at McDonalds after school for dinner, and I get a salad there," I explain. "When I eat breakfast, a bowl of fruits is enough. So my mom doesn't know because she's not there to see."

"Your dad?"

I freeze, look down at my feet and then back at him. "Died last year from lung cancer."

"Oh," he says. "I'm sorry."

I shrug, pretending to be okay. "Not your fault."

The bell rings, and he says, "Look, we obviously don't have time now, but do you think that I can talk to you later?"

"Busy," I say, grabbing my books.

"When I say later, it doesn't necessarily have to be today," he says. "Tomorrow?"

"Well, I'm going to see you tomorrow here at school again, so I don't really have a choice, do I?" I say.

He smiles. "No. I guess you don't."

"He did *what?*"

I sigh as I look through the clothing rack. "Rose, all we did was have a conversation."

"Yeah," she says. "A deep one. And he said you're special and that he likes the fact that you're a bookworm, *and* that he wants to see you again. And that he was thinking about you."

"He said that I'm half his friend. I wouldn't exactly call that deep," I say. "Plus, it's not like he was asking me for a date or anything."

"What if he did?"

I stare at her. "Rose, I just met him!"

She shrugs and goes back to looking at the clothes. "But if you get to know him, then would you?"

"It would depend what he's like, of course," I say. "And so far he comes off as nosy and strange."

"What kind of nosy?"

"Worrying type of nosy. And curious."

"Isn't that a good thing?" she says.

"How so?"

"You're curious. He's curious. He's strange. You're strange."

"Hey!"

"A good strange," she says. "Like me."

"Other people see you as perfect."

"And how do you see me?"

"Crazy."

"And that's the same way they would see me if they got to know me."

"Whatever," I mutter and pass her a dress I think she'll like.

She examines the dress and keeps talking. "Anyway, he seems like a nice guy."

"I guess," I say. "But how does he even know you?"

"You're not the only person I talk to, Marissa," she smiles.

"But when *did* you talk to him?"

"Oh, it was a while ago," she says. "When we were in sixth grade, we were locker neighbors. I talked to him sometimes. Rarely, though. These days we just say hi, and that's about it."

"Oh," I say.

"Do you think he's cute?"

"*What?*"

"Yeah, like," she turns to me and uses her hands to make a square shape around her face. "*A-cute.*"

I roll my eyes. "No, he is not square-shaped."

She hits me with a shirt she is holding. "Don't try to change the subject!"

"I'm not!" I say. "You asked if he was acute, and I'm saying he's not a square."

"You know what I mean," she says.

"I'm not sure I do."

She hits me with a shirt again. "You're annoying."

"Yet you still love me."

"Not at the moment," she jokes and throws a dress at me that lands on my head.

I pull it off and look at it. "This is actually pretty cute, thank you."

"You're welcome," she says and begins heading towards the dressing room. "Now are we going to try these on?"

I shrug. "Might as well."

We each go into one of the stalls and hang up the outfits we picked out. We agreed to show each other it every time we try one on.

"But how about you?" I ask.

"What?"

"Anyone you like?"

She pauses. "No."

"Really?" I ask, surprised.

"Why is that so shocking?" she says.

"Because you used to have the biggest crush on some guy," I say.

"He was not *some guy,*" she says. "Are you done?"

"I know that he wasn't *some guy,*" I reply. "I'm just saying that because I can't remember his name. And yeah, I am."

I step out of the dressing room I was in, and she does too. "Wasn't his name Andy, or something?" I say. "Oh, and what do you think of this?" I spin around in a full circle to show her. I'm wearing the green dress she threw at me.

"It actually looks really pretty," she says. "You should get it. Is it too fancy for church? And his name was Andrew."

"I don't really go to church anymore, Rose. After ... well, never mind. And I remember, he went by Andy."

"Whatever. That was back in Junior High," she says. "What do you think of this?"

She spins in a circle also but adding a little dance to it, and I laugh.

"It's nice," I say. "The blue brings out your eyes. And Junior High was a year ago."

"I mean seventh grade."

"Okay, then two years ago."

"He doesn't even go to our school anymore."

"How would you know? There's like a thousand people in our school. So he could be there, and you don't even know it. Could be that you just don't have any classes with him."

"Are you going to buy that dress?"

I look down at the dress then back up at her. "I don't know. Should I?"

"Yes, you should," she says. "How much is it?"

"Check the tag." I turn my back to her and she checks the price tag.

"Ooh … How much money did you bring today?"

"About eighty."

"Unless you plan on using all your money, you can't get it."

"Oh come on!" I go back into the dressing room and check the tag for myself. Over seventy dollars.

"But it's so pretty!" I say.

"I know! And it looks great on you," Rose agrees.

"How much is the dress that you tried on?"

"Fifty," she says. "But I'm not getting it. I might find something cheaper and cuter along the way."

"Well, I never find something cute," I say. "This could be my only chance to get something like this."

"So are you?" she says. "You could always get an extra shift next week."

We both work at this drugstore near my house. I only work there three times a week so it wouldn't kill me if I worked there five times a week.

"I guess that's true," I say.

I hear her door open as she steps out of her dressing room, and she says, "So are you going to get it?"

"No."

She immediately knows it's not worth arguing by the sound of my voice, so she just says, "Hurry up, would you?"

"Okay, just wait." I open the door to my dressing room and go towards her, hopping on one foot since I'm still trying to get my other shoe on.

She stands there with her hand on her hip. "How long does it take for you to put a shoe on?"

"Not long," I say, standing up straight. I finally got my shoe on. "You're just impatient."

"I am not!"

"Yes, you are."

"No."

"Yes."

"No."

"Yes."

"No!"

"Yes, you are."

She's quiet for a minute. "Okay, just a little."

"Uh-huh …"

We walk in silence for a little while, and then her stomach growls. "I'm hungry," she says.

"Obviously," I say.

"What's that supposed to mean?" she says.

"Your stomach just growled," I point out. "So it's obvious."

"I see your point," she says. "Let's get some ice cream."

"Go ahead," I say. "But I'm good."

She stops and looks at me. "Marissa, you *have* to start eating."

"I do eat."

"Not just fruits and water and salad!" she says. "If you had it as a side, or if you ate more of it, or if you didn't skip one meal a day, then okay. But no, you eat like one salad and one fruit."

"But I'm still eating!"

"Not enough!" she says. "It's not healthy!"

"Now you sound like Leon."

"If he said that, then he's right! It's okay to eat something sweet every once in a while," she says. "An unhealthy meal doesn't make you an unhealthy person."

"I don't have unhealthy meals, though," I say.

"If you don't eat enough, then that counts as unhealthy."

"Okay, you know what?" I say. "Fine, you win. I'll eat it."

She smiles. "Good."

In the end, I buy my own and pretend to eat it but throw it away at the first garbage I can see when she's not looking. I don't need her worrying about me.

CHAPTER THREE

"Just in time."

Graham smiles as I sit down next to him in the library. I put my books on the table and smile back. "Yeah. I don't want to be late like *someone*."

"That was once!"

"Sure it was."

"Whatever," he mutters, but I can tell that he's trying not to laugh. "So anyway, today we can only study for thirty minutes because I have somewhere to be—"

"Wow, Graham, congratulations!"

"Wait, what?"

"You finally have a social life!"

He glares at me, and I laugh. "This isn't all I do, you know!" he says.

I continue to laugh, and eventually, he has to chuckle. "What's so funny?"

"You!" I say. "How do you do that?"

"Do what?"

"There're not many people that can make me laugh," I say. "And you can. And I just met you!"

"Correction: I have been tutoring you for two weeks now."

"Exactly," I say. "I just met you. So how do you do that?"

"I don't know," he shrugs. "But I'm happy that I can make you laugh."

"And why is that?"

"One, because you have a funny laugh and it makes me laugh …"

I punch him in the shoulder.

"Two, because I have this game with my friend about making people laugh and smile."

"A game?"

"Yeah," he says. "If we make someone smile, like a big sincere smile, not a forced one, that's one point. Now if we make someone laugh, that's two points. And so far I'm winning."

"How?" I ask.

"Because every time I tutor you, I get you to laugh, and I don't even know how I do it—"

"Because you're nerdy and weird, and that passes as hilarious to me."

"Shut up."

I laugh again.

"See, there're two more points! And I'm starting to think that making *you* laugh gets some bonus points."

"What? Why?"

"Because my friend talks about you *all* the time," he says. "And everyday when we count the points and I say that I made you laugh or smile, he gets kinda red in the face and mutters something like, 'Shut up, Graham,' or 'I could do that too.'"

"You have a weird friend."

"Like a good weird?"

"I probably don't even know him," I say. "So how should I know?"

"*Probably*," he repeats.

"What?"

"You *probably* don't know him," he says. "But you could."

"The only people I hang out with, or let alone even talk to, would be you, Rose, or Leon."

"That's him."

"*Leon?*"

"Yeah," he says. "It's odd that he goes by Leon."

"Isn't that his name?" I say.

"Yes," he says. "Wait, no. Kind of."

"What's that supposed to mean?" I ask.

"That's a nickname," he says. "It's only half his name. Literally. It's the first half of his name."

"Then what's his full name?"

"He hasn't told you?" he asks surprised, and I shake my head. "He said he did!"

"No," I say. "When I met him, he introduced himself as Leon Graeme."

"He didn't even tell you his middle name?" he asks.

"What did I just say?" I reply. "Now are you going to tell me?"

"His full name is Leondre Marcman Graeme," he says.

"*Leondre?*" I repeat.

"What did I just say?" he mimics me, smirking.

I jokingly glare at him, and he smiles. He checks his watch and chuckles. "You're actually very smart."

"Why do you say that?"

"Because we've spent almost the entire thirty minutes talking about your laugh and Leon's real name."

I laugh. "How much time do we have left?"

"Ten minutes."

"Do you want to leave early?"

"That's another reason why you're smart," he says. "You know that I have to be somewhere, so you know that it's better if I get a head start. Therefore, you can see that I want to leave."

"Oh, so you do understand!"

He smiles, rips a piece of paper from his notebook and writes something down.

"Here," he says. "Since I didn't tutor you today, then just text me or call me if you need help with your homework, okay?" "Okay," I take the piece of paper, and he stands up to leave, and so do I. "Wait, this has two numbers on it."

"Oh, yeah," he says. "One of them is Leondre's."

"Well, how am I supposed to know which is which?"

"You'll just have to call them both," he smiles and turns to leave. "Bye!"

"Oh, come on Graham!" I say. "Why?"

"He paid me to do that!" he answers without turning around. "Later!"

Leon paid Graham to do this? Are you kidding me?

Am I being pranked?

I look around for any sign that I'm being filmed. Besides the school security cameras, there's nothing.

Wait.

What if the school security cameras *are* the live cameras for a prank?

I really *do* have an overactive imagination.

After school, I just go to the drugstore to see if I can work today to get paid extra.

I walk in and the bell above the door jingles.

The person at the counter turns and smiles at me. "Good afternoon, Marissa!" he says. "How are you?"

I go behind the counter, put my skateboard down, and smile at him. "You're about to ask me something, aren't you, Marcus?"

"*What?*" he says. "How dare you accuse me of such a thing!"

I roll my eyes at him. "Drop the act, and just come out with it."

"Okay, okay," he sighs. "I need you to start working here at least four times a week. Please?"

"Do I get paid more?"

"If you want to be," he says with a smile.

"Of course, I do!"

"Okay, then yes, you'll get paid more."

"How much more?"

"Well, $10 per hour. How about that?"

Marcus works full time here because he's eighteen and has nothing better to do. Working three more hours and being paid more is exactly what I need, so I take the offer with no hesitation.

"Okay."

"Okay, then you'll be working from Monday to Thursday every week from now on," he says. "And since today is Thursday," he tosses me a washcloth. "You start now."

I start to wipe down the counter while he sorts out some other stuff.

I finish and walk over to him. "You know, it's funny."

"What is?" he asks.

"I came here to ask if I could work a few extra hours, and you gave me exactly that right when I walked in." I grab a box full of candy and begin putting all of the stuff in place.

"So I agreed to pay you more for *nothing?*" he says.

"Too late to turn back now," I reply. "A deal is a deal."

"I see your point," he says, and then there's the sound of a bell, but I don't look up. It's just another customer.

"I got the soda," a voice says.

"I'll get the rest," another replies.

"Since you're going to be working here more often now," Marcus says to me. "Then you should meet our usual Thursday customers."

Now I look up to see whom these 'usual Thursday customers' are.

What?

No.

Just my luck.

"Marissa?" Leon says and walks over to me. "I didn't know you work here!"

"I didn't know you even came here," I say. "Hey, Graham."

"'Sup?" he says and smiles at me.

"How long have you been working here?" Leon asks.

"About a year or so, from Monday to Wednesday," I reply. I finish and head to the counter to put the empty box away and grab another one with chips.

"How often do you guys come here?" I ask.

Leon shrugs. "Every Thursday afternoon." He glances at the box I'm holding, then back at me. "Here, let me help you."

"No, you really don't—" he takes the box from me. "Okay."

I take the stuff from the box and put them in place while he holds it. "Why weren't you at school today?" I ask.

"So you thought of me." He smiles. "That's one step closer to us being friends, you know."

"I never said that."

"But you noticed that I wasn't at school today," he replies. "And if you noticed, then you must've wondered where I was and why. And that would mean that you thought of me."

"Just answer my question," I say.

"I was helping my little brother with something," he says.

"What's his name?"

"Xander," he says. "He's a really good kid."

"Leondre and Xander," I think out loud. "Does he look like you?"

"People say he's like a mini-me," he says. "Wait, hold on a second. Did you just say 'Leondre'?"

"Yeah," I answer. "That's your name, isn't it?"

"Yes, but," he replies. "How do you know that?"

"How do I know that your full name is Leondre Marcman Graeme?" I say teasingly.

"And you call me a stalker."

I hit him over the head with a pack of chips I'm holding. "I'm not, unlike you!" I reply, putting the chips in place. "Graham told me."

"Graham!" Leon yells.

Graham walks over to where we are. "You told him, didn't you?" he asks.

"I honestly don't see why it matters," I say.

"He doesn't like his full name," Graham says.

"And why didn't you mention that earlier?" I ask.

He shrugs. "I forgot."

I turn to Leon. "Why don't you like your full name?"

"I just don't."

"I really like that name, so I don't know why you don't."

"You like it?"

"It sounds cool," I say. "I mean, Leondre Marcman Graeme sounds like a celebrity or something. So I like it."

Graham elbows Leondre. "See? I told you."

I smile, take the empty box from Leon and put it back under the counter. "Do you guys always stay here this long?"

"Yes, we do," Leon says at the same time that Graham says, "Nope."

"So which one of you do I believe?" I ask. "And you have to pay for that." I point at the bag of chips that Graham is eating.

"Oh yeah," he turns to Leon. "Did you get the water and soda?"

"I'll get it right now," he says and heads over to the fridge.

I grab a popcorn bag and start eating it as Graham crosses his arms and leans on the counter top. My mind starts over thinking: I shouldn't be eating this. It has too many calories, and it's way too unhealthy, but I'm really, really hungry. I'll go running after, even though I'm weak. I will eat only once tomorrow. And it would have to be a light salad.

"He got distracted," Graham says, bringing my attention back to him.

"By what?" I ask, completely oblivious.

"You," he rolls his eyes. "Duh."

"Very funny," I say.

"You think I'm joking?" he says. "Marissa, I know you're slow, but there's no way you're *this* slow."

I throw some of my popcorn at him. "I'm not slow. I'm just saying that he either has ADD or he got distracted by something really interesting to him that we see as plain."

"Like I said, you."

I throw more popcorn at him. "Okay, you're annoying."

"And yet," he says. "I'm still your friend."

"Is it really that easy?" I ask.

"What?"

"To make a friend," I say. "Is it?"

"If it's hard, then that's not a friend," he says. "That's either some jerk that likes attention, or it's someone who wants to be left alone. Now if it's the first, walk away. If it's the second, then keep on trying. Because then maybe you'll get to them, and they won't want to be alone anymore."

"And what if it's easy?"

He smiles. "That's a real friend that'll hang around for a while."

"How about the second one?"

"Then that's also a real friend who shouldn't let go of someone who tried so hard to be with them. If they do, you should tell them to piss off before they get a chance to."

I laugh, and Leon comes back with the soda.

"When do you get off?" he asks as they both pull out some money.

"Leon, I just started working a half hour ago," I say. "I still have another hour."

"Can't you see if you can get off early?"

"Why?"

They look at each other and smile, and then they turn back to me.

"We want to show you something," Graham says.

"What do you want to show me?" I ask.

"It's a surprise," Leon says.

I sigh. "Marcus probably isn't going to let me."

"We know Marcus," Graham says. "And he knows and trusts us. So just try. We already invited Rose to go."

Now I'm surprised, but I try not to show it. "And is she going?"

"She's going to meet us there," he says.

"Oh, so she can know, and I can't."

"Well, she's been there before," Leon says.

"How has she been there before?"

"Do you really need to know everything?"

"Yes."

Leon looks over at Graham and Graham shrugs. "She really does, or else she won't shut up," he simply says, shoving some more chips in his mouth.

I throw another handful of popcorn at him.

"You're going to have to clean that up, you know!" he says.

"I don't care," I say. "It's pretty easy to sweep popcorn up."

"Anyway," Leon interrupts. "She was the one who told us about the place."

"And how come she's never told me?"

"She said that you probably wouldn't want to go anyway."

"And she's right," I say.

"You've never even been there!"

"Don't plan to."

"Please?" He's practically begging now, but I don't know why. What difference will it make if I do or don't go?

"Okay, fine," I say. "But Marcus probably won't let me."

"You can at least try."

I put my popcorn down on the counter and go into the room that Marcus is in.

"Hey, Marcus?" I say. "I was wondering if maybe—"

"Nope," he says.

"*THANK YOU!*" I whisper. He nods and winks at me.

I walk out the door back to the counter and find that Leon and Graham are both already waiting with my sweater on the counter.

"Let's go?" Graham says.

"I didn't even tell you if I *could* go!" I reply.

"Can you?"

"Nope."

"Aww, why?" Leon asks.

"Boss said. And I'm in the middle of my shift!"

"When do you get off?"

I check my watch. "'Bout an hour or so."

"Then we'll wait," he says and jumps up on the counter.

"What? But ..."

Graham shrugs and says, "Is there a place I could nap here?" I sigh and point to the back. "Sweet," he grins at me and goes through the door. I'm pretty sure that Marcus is going to make him sleep on the table instead of the bed we keep there for whenever one of us wants to take a break, which actually happens quite often.

Much to my surprise, they're both quite patient. Leon barely says anything, and instead plays something on his phone and puts some headphones on. I check on Graham twice, and he's totally knocked out (on the table, just as I assumed). I give Marcus a suspicious look.

"Believe it or not, I offered the bed," is all he says.

An hour and fifteen minutes later, he finally lets me off the hook, and I toss the washcloth at his face.

"I'll pay you tomorrow," he says. "Now shoo."

I turn to Graham, who Leon woke up by tipping over the table, and ask, "Where are we even going?"

"It's a surprise," he says.

"Yeah, but still."

"No questions, just go." Leon cuts me off as he grabs my sweater from the counter, and Graham shoves me out the door.

"Okay, okay," I say, stopping once we get outside. "Now, can I have my sweater? I'm cold."

"Here you go." Leon drapes my sweater over my shoulders and makes sure it doesn't fall.

"Thanks," I mutter. "So how far is this place?"

"Not far," Graham says. "We can walk there from here. It's about a block away."

"I've lived here my whole life, and there is not a single good place around here that's that close by," I say.

Leon shrugs. "That depends on how you look at it."

"What?"

He tries to explain. "Places are like people. It seems boring if you only focus on the flaws. But then if you focus on the good parts, you could have found the best thing that you will *ever* find in your *entire life.*"

"Now if Leon is done trying to tell us the meaning of life, we should go on our way," Graham says and then starts walking down the sidewalk without waiting for a response, knowing that we'll follow.

Leon laughs and runs after Graham. "I was just saying!" he says, and then jumps on Graham's back, almost causing them both to fall on the concrete.

"Hey!" Graham laughs and throws Leon off of him, causing them both to almost bump into me, but I move out of the way at the last second.

"Are we going?" I ask. "And if we are, will I be third-wheeling the whole way there?"

"Sorry," Leon chuckles, straightening up. "Sorry. Let's go."

He motions for Graham to follow, and he does, and we finally go on our way.

We walk a few steps without talking, each of us lost in our own thoughts until my curiosity gets the best of me, and I break the silence.

"So," I say. "What's this place like?"

Leon thinks about it for a moment, and then says, "It's … not the kind of place that you would expect a bunch of teenagers to hang out."

I pause. "That doesn't exactly help."

"I know," he says. "But I'm not supposed to give out hints."

I groan. "You guys must really *love* to torture me."

"We don't, actually," Graham says. "But it's so easy that we don't even know that we're doing it."

"What's that supposed to mean?"

"Why do you need to know?"

"Just tell me already!"

"You just answered your own question."

His answer takes me by surprise so that I'm quiet for a while. "What?" I finally say.

"It's easy to torture curious people," he says. "Just say that there's something you need to tell them, but don't tell them right away. They'll spend the rest of the time trying to figure it out until you say something."

"And you're very curious," Leon adds. "So it's not on purpose. It just happens."

"Blame genetics," I say.

"Nah, it was just God. Turn this corner," Leon says, pointing ahead of us.

I look at him a little confused from what Leon just said as we walk towards the last turn.

"Wait."

I stop in the middle of my tracks and turn to Graham, who told us to stop.

"What?" I ask.

"You have to close your eyes."

"Why?"

"Just do it."

I close my eyes.

"Marissa," Leon says.

"Yes?" I reply.

"Stop peeking."

"But I'm not!"

"*Marissa.*"

I stop peeking.

"Good," he says. "We'll lead you, okay? And just in case, I'm going to tie Graham's scarf around your eyes."

"How do I know that you won't lead me into a pole?" I ask.

"And why would I do that to you?" he replies.

"Leondre, I've only known you for a week," I say.

"If I wanted to prank you or hurt you, I already would've done it," he says while he ties the final knot. "All done."

I'm about to argue that this is ridiculous and that there's no need for me to be blindfolded, but then they begin to push me ahead to whatever place we're going to.

They give me directions, like "Watch out," or "Turn here," and eventually, "Step down," which means we're about to cross the street.

"If I get hit by a car," I say. "It's on you."

I hear Leon move and stand right next to me on my right, and he puts his hand on my shoulder. "You won't," he says into my ear. "And if you do, since it'll be our fault, then we'll get hit too."

I can tell by the tone of his voice that he doesn't believe that anything will happen, and I'm once again about to protest when he shoves me forward across the street.

After a few seconds, he says, "Step up," and we're on the sidewalk again, and I relax.

"You have trust issues," Graham says as Leon begins to untie the blindfold.

"You have no idea," I reply. "By the way, it's getting late and it is dark already. Soon I have to go home."

Leon ignores my complaints and pulls the blindfold off, and I'm standing in the middle of a tiny parking lot in front of a frozen yogurt shop.

"Here?" I say. "This place is really rundown. Almost no one comes here!"

"*Almost* no one," Graham says. "Except for us. Have you ever been here?"

"A few times in eighth grade," I say. "And back then this shop had already been sitting here for ten years."

"Either way, it's closed right now," Leon points out.

"Then what was the point of coming?" I ask.

"We hang out in the parking lot," Graham says.

"Seriously?" I ask.

"Yeah."

I turn around and see Rose leaning against the brick wall of the building.

"Did you guys bring the soda?" she asks and begins walking towards us.

Graham opens his backpack and tosses her a can, and she catches it.

"What's so great about this place?" I ask.

"Marissa, do you remember what I said earlier?" Leon asks.

"Yes."

"Well, right now, you're looking at all the flaws," he says. "You're seeing how—how old this place is. How it's close to being shut down and no one comes here. But look at all the good stuff."

I look around, then back at him. "Like what?"

"Like how this place is in the middle of nowhere," he says, and then looks up at the sky and yells at the top of his lungs, "AND WE CAN BE AS LOUD AS WE WANT!" he turns back to me. "And no one can ever complain. Also, if you look up," he points at the sky. "You can see the stars. Oh, the creativity of a Creator behind all of that."

It is the second time Leon mentions God in such a natural way. Now I'm really intrigued by this boy. I look at where he's pointing and see that he's right. I can see everything. If I had a telescope, I might even be able to see one of the planets. The sky is clear and it is so beautiful!

"Do you know any constellations?" Leon asks.

"Only the Big Dipper," I answer. "But everyone knows that one."

He shakes his head. "Not everyone," he says and smiles. "So which one is it?"

I look up at the sky and search for it. "That one," I say, pointing up at him. "It goes straight, then curves downward like a hook."

"Right there?" he points also, putting his hand next to mine, making sure that he sees the right one.

"Yeah," I say.

I put my hand down and so does he, and for a second, it's so quiet, you can hear crickets.

"Have you ever talked to the stars?" he suddenly asks, turning to me.

"What?" I say, surprised.

"Like, just randomly say things," he says. "They're actually very good at keeping secrets."

I laugh a bit. "They should be."

"I only talk to them when there's no one else to talk to," he says. "When I've already told Graham everything, but I feel like I have to tell someone else, I don't want to talk to myself. That makes everything worse. And it makes me sound like a loser."

"And talking to stars doesn't?" I joke.

He smiles. "I think it's better," he looks back at the sky. "Can you find the second star to the right?"

I turn to my left where the moon is at the moment and look for the first star on the right. "There's one ... and there's the second." I nod towards it, and he sees it too.

"What's your favorite quote in that book?" he asks.

"Quote? In *Peter Pan*?" I ask, and he nods. I think about it for a second and then say, "*You must not feel sorry for her. She was one of the kind that likes to grow up.*"

"That one?" he asks. "I like that one, but ... it kind of makes me sad."

"Same here," I reply. "But at the same time, it makes me happy."

He doesn't question it. He just nods and looks at the ground.

"What's yours?" I ask.

He doesn't even hesitate before telling me, "I think mine would have to be, '*Wendy, oh Wendy, while you're sleeping in your silly bed, you might be flying about with me, saying funny things to the stars.*'"

I scoff, and he chuckles. "Ironic, right?"

He smiles at me, and I smile back, and I'm thinking about how I have never met someone so different and apart from me yet so close and the same. He seems so familiar, but not as someone that I have just met this week, but as someone who's been around my whole life, but I never bothered to say hello to.

Neither of us say anything for a moment, and we're just enjoying each other's company until I decide to break the silence by asking, "Do you believe in that kind of stuff? Magic?"

"No, I don't," he says. "But I do believe that all the stars have a name. And that someone created them. Almost everything has to have a beginning, right? And I highly doubt that some big rocks exploding in space could think up all of this."

"You mean, you actually believe in God?" I ask.

He looks at me, furrowing his eyebrows, confused. "Of course. Don't you?"

I hesitate. "Kind of, I guess."

"Well, why do you think I talk to stars?" He points to them again, only for a moment, and then puts his arm down again. "I know there's someone beyond them."

I'm about to respond when I hear, "Oh my gosh, Graham, no."

We turn around to see Graham shaking a closed can of soda, and Rose with her head in her hands.

"What're you doing?" Leon asks them.

"Graham decided to explode some Sprite cans for absolutely no reason whatsoever," Rose explains.

"How many has he exploded?" I ask.

"None," she says, but then mumbles, "*Yet.*"

"Graham," Leon says. "Why?"

Graham stops shaking the can. "Look, man, I'm bored. This is the only thing that I can think of to do at the moment."

He puts the can on the floor and gets ready to open it. "One, two …"

"Graham—"

"Three!"

He pulls off the top and steps back as fast as he can, but we don't. The soda sprays all over us, even though Leon used his sweater to try to block it.

Surprisingly enough, it only gets on Graham's jeans and sneakers, but it sprays on my face and even my hair. Some got on my shirt, but not much, thanks to Leon's sweater. On the other hand, it got all over Rose.

"Dude!" I yell. "Why—"

"I already told you I'm bored," he cuts me off. "That's why."

"Well, what a coincidence ..." we turn to see Rose shaking another soda can and walking over to Graham. "So am I."

Before Graham can react, he's hit with a gush of orange soda all over his face.

When she finally puts the can down, he takes off his glasses and starts wiping them on his shirt.

"Nice," he says.

"Thank you," she replies.

"Congratulations," Leon says. "You have accomplished getting us all messed up and sticky with soda."

"Guess I can check that off my bucket list," Graham says sarcastically.

I roll my eyes and reach down to grab a water bottle from my purse on the floor.

"Are you really going to do that?" Leon asks.

I nod. "This could help wash it off. And what's the worst it can do? It can't ruin my outfit," I gesture at my clothes. "Too late for that."

I take off the bottle cap, close my eyes, and tip it upside down over my head, and the water pours down on me.

"Do you have any more water?" I hear Rose ask.

"Yeah, here," Graham says, and I pull the water bottle away from my head and open my eyes to see Rose open another water bottle and pour it over her head.

"Are you going to do it?" I ask the guys, grabbing another water bottle.

"Nope," Graham says.

"I'm good," Leon agrees.

"Okay," I say. "That makes this more fun."

"Huh?"

I sneak up behind Leon and dump the water over him.

"Oh!" He yells. "What—"

"Keep your mouth closed, you might drown," I joke.

"Cut it out!" he turns around and tries to take the water bottle away, but I fight back.

He's behind me holding one of my arms and trying to catch my other arm holding the water bottle, but I tip it back behind me, and it continues to drench his hair and shirt.

Once the bottle is empty, I turn around and throw it at his head.

"Ow!" he yells.

"There's no way that hurt," I say.

"Oh, yeah?" he picks up the empty water bottle and throws it at me, but misses completely. "You have horrible aim," I say.

"In case you haven't noticed," he says, stepping closer. "My hair is kind of covering my face."

I laugh because he has a point. His hair is wet and matted down, so it covers his eyes, and I can imagine how hard it is to see. I reach up and move his bangs so he can see, and he smiles. "I could've done that myself," he says.

"Doesn't seem like it," I reply. I turn away and grab another bottle. "Now it's Graham's turn."

"About that ..."

I look past Leon and cannot control my laughter. Graham is standing there with Rose behind him, with not just a bottle of water, but a plastic bag full of it. I'm just in time to see her open the bag and Graham gets soaked.

"Oh, that water is *cold!*" he shouts.

"Cold?" I repeat, then look at Rose.

"Oh, I got it from the faucet," she says.

"What faucet?"

She points to the frozen yogurt shop, and I see water gushing out from a small sink.

"And that water is *ice cold*," Rose finishes.

"You don't say!" Graham yells sarcastically.

Rose pulls out another water bottle, opens it, and squeezes it in the middle, and the water shoots out in his face.

"I just cleaned my glasses," he says.

"Oh, well," she says, putting the cap back on.

The wind blows in our direction, and I shiver, suddenly cold. My sweater is no use. It's soaked too.

"We're going to end up catching pneumonia," Leon says, reading my mind.

"No, we won't," Rose says and reaches down to her backpack on the floor, pulling out a blanket. "I only have one, but it's pretty big, so we can share it."

Seeing as we have no other option, we drape the blanket over our shoulders and sit down on the concrete. Graham is next to Rose, Rose is next to me, and I'm next to Leon. We all stare up at the sky.

"So what was it," Rose whispers to me. "That you said earlier?"

"About what?" I reply, turning to her.

"You and Leon," she says. "You guys were talking about stars."

I look over at Leon, and he shakes his head. He doesn't want me to tell her about that whole talking to stars thing.

"The Big Dipper," I tell her. "Right up there." I point up at the constellation and trace it with my finger. I feel like maybe if I reach a little farther, I can literally touch the sky.

Another gust of wind blows in our direction, and I sink a little farther back into the blanket. Leon tries to adjust it so I can be warmer, and it actually helps a bit, and I gratefully pull a little more of it around my arms.

"How do you guys know each other?" I suddenly ask.

"I already told you," Rose says. "Middle school. Locker neighbors. Simple hellos."

"You guys seem a lot closer than that," I point out.

"No, see I've known *Graham* for a long time," she explains. "I never introduced you guys to each other because I know that socializing isn't exactly your thing."

"How long has she been like that?" Graham asks.

"Since eighth grade," Rose responds, then turns back to me. "Anyway, I told Graham about this place, and he told Leon, and I knew that he would want to invite you, and since Marcus knows them, I knew that you would be allowed to come, and there you go. I knew that you had already met Graham since he's your tutor, and Leon because you told me about that lunch thing—"

"You *told* her?" Leon cuts her off.

"We're *best friends,* Leondre," I say. "We tell each other everything."

"Please don't call me Leondre," he says. "And if you guys tell each other everything, how come Rose never told you about us meeting?"

"Rephrase: we tell each other everything that's *important,"* I correct myself. "Just saying 'hi' and 'bye' to someone, or just meeting someone isn't very important."

"Yet our conversation was important somehow," he points out.

"Because you would not *shut up* about my book and my lunch," I snap.

"I was just worried," he says. "An apple isn't enough for lunch!"

"Well, it is for me."

"Marissa—"

"Why does it matter?"

"Because I—"

"Gosh, you guys fight like a married couple," Graham interrupts.

"I'm sorry, Graham, but do you want to get water poured down your shirt again?" I retort, and he puts his hands up in surrender. "Didn't think so."

"We should bring a telescope out here next time," Rose says.

"Next time?" I say.

"Of course," she says. "This isn't just a one-time thing. No way. In my opinion, if something good happens, and you can do it again, don't hesitate."

"She has a point," Leon says.

"Guys, I have work," I say.

"So do I," Rose says. "So we'll just go after work. Please?"

"Please?" Leon begs.

"Please?" Graham joins in, after Rose elbows him.

"Okay, fine," I say. "But right now, I'm going home, because I'm cold and need to take a shower."

I stand up, and so do they. "Call your mom," Rose says. "See if you can sleepover today."

"Yeah, like she'll agree to that," I say sarcastically.

"Tell her that I'll make you do your homework," she suggests.

I shrug. "Good point."

I pull out my phone and dial her number.

"Hi, Marissa," my mom answers. "I'm going to be working late today."

I'm really not surprised. My mom works at a hospital as a nurse, and she stays late at least three times a week. Usually more.

"Oh, then do you think that I can sleepover Rose's house?" I ask.

"Where are you right now?" she asks.

"In the parking lot of a Frozen Yogurt shop," I reply.

She doesn't even question that. "Is Rose there?"

"Yes."

"You don't have any extra clothes," she points out.

I look over at Rose, and she nods.

"She'll let me borrow some," I say into the phone.

"What about your homework?"

"Mom, you know she's the one who always pushes me to do it," I say.

She thinks it over. "That is true."

"Yeah."

"Okay, then yes, you can sleepover her house," she says.

"Thanks, Mom."

"Have fun."

"We will."

"Love you."

"Love you too."

I hang up and turn to Rose, who's already putting on her backpack. "Come on," she says.

I start to go after her when Leon stops me. "Wait," he says. "We're still going to meet here tomorrow, right?"

"Maybe," I say, and before he can say anything else, I walk away with Rose.

Once we're out of earshot, Rose blurts out, "I ship it."

"What?"

"You and Leon," she says. "I ship it. Which means, I think you guys should be together."

"I know what it means more than you do," I say. "But no, don't say that."

"Why not?"

"Um, because I just met him!"

"Well, he used to go to our middle school, but you never talked to him."

"Either way, that still means that I just met him."

"He used to hang out with Andrew," she says. "It was him, Leon, and Graham, in one little group of friends. Now he has that huge group of friends."

"Acquaintances," I mutter under my breath.

"What?"

"Not friends," I say. "Acquaintances."

CHAPTER FOUR

Three hours later, we're sitting on Rose's bedroom floor wearing pajamas and playing 'Would You Rather?' and as it turns out, Rose wasn't kidding about making me do my homework.

"Okay, would you rather . . ." I try to think of a question. "Sacrifice yourself to save your family and friends, or sacrifice your family and friends to save yourself?"

"Sacrifice my friends and family," she jokes.

I give an overdramatic gasp and throw a pillow at her, and she laughs.

"I'm just kidding!" she says.

"I know," I reply. "If you weren't, I'd kick you out of your own house."

"Well!" she says sarcastically, and I laugh and take a sip of my water.

"Okay, okay, my turn," she looks up at the ceiling as if it will suddenly give her something to ask me. "Oh! I got one! Would you rather date Graham or Leon?"

"What kind of question is that?" I ask.

"Just answer it!" she says.

"Next question," I say.

"One of the rules of the game is that you have to answer *all* questions," she says, and then points at me. "And you're the one who made that rule."

"We're in the twenty-first century, and they still haven't invented time machines," I say. "Come on, America!"

"Just answer!"

"Fine! Um …" I trail off.

"So?" she demands.

"Calm yourself! You really are impatient."

"Marissa!"

"Okay, Leon, I guess," I answer.

"I knew it!" she yells and jumps up.

"Knew *what?*" I say.

"You *like* him!" Rose squeals.

"Oh, my gosh," I say. "Rose, we've been through this!"

"You just admitted it!" she says.

"You made me answer the question!" I say. "I had no choice!"

"But you chose him over Graham."

"So?"

"So," she says. "Graham is a super good guy, and you still chose *Leon* over him. Like, *I* wouldn't do that!"

I stand up, pick up a pillow and start hitting her with it.

"Hey!" she yells. "I'm just being honest!"

"The *one* time you decide not to sugarcoat something," I say. "It had to be *now?*"

She laughs and falls back onto her bed. "I'm always honest with you."

"Sadly."

I jump onto the bed next to her, and we stare up at the violet ceiling of her bedroom.

"Rose?" I say.

"Yeah?" she replies.

"What's wrong with us?" I ask.

"Everything,"

"What's *not* wrong with us?"

She's quiet for a minute, thinking it over, neither of us looking away from the ceiling, somehow fascinated by just a wall.

She takes a breath, obviously tired, and then answers.

"Nothing," she says. "We're both ... mad."

"Is that a good thing?" I ask.

"We embrace our madness while others deny it," she says. "I don't see how it can be a bad thing."

"Wake up, Marissa. We're going to be late."

I groan and roll over onto my right side, away from the voice calling me.

"Yeah, I know," Rose says. "I don't want to go either. But we don't really have a choice, do we?'

"Yes, we do," I mutter and pull the blankets over my head. "We can lie here and fall asleep again into unconsciousness and numbness and forget the world."

"I want to do that as much as you," she says. "But we can't because my dad will drag us to school even in our pajamas, so get up because I don't feel like going to school looking hideous."

I turn and look at her. "What happened to your mom?" I ask.

"Had to leave early for work," she says. "Now get up."

I sit up and rub my eyes. "Gosh, I'm exhausted."

"We stayed up half the night," she says. "What do you expect?"

I force myself to get up and get ready, and head to the bathroom to brush my hair. Rose gasps.

"What?"

"Nothing," she says quickly. "It's just ... your arms are so thin."

"They've always been like that." I shrug.

She simply purses her lips, not entirely convinced, nods and walks away.

She heads to her drawers. "What outfit do you want to borrow?"

"Any T-shirt that's not pink, jeans, and a hoodie," I say. "I have my own sneakers."

"The rest of your clothes aren't dry yet?" she asks.

I shake my head. "Not yet."

"Here you go," she throws a red T-shirt onto the bed with the rest of the clothes. "You can keep the shirt. I never use it."

"Good, because then that way I won't feel guilty since I was going to take it anyway," I say.

"Ha-ha," she says dryly. "Get dressed."

"Yes, mother," I say sarcastically.

We get dressed, say bye to Rose's dad, and then head outside to wait for the bus.

"Do we have any tests in English class today?" she asks as we sit on the curb.

"No, I don't think so," I say. "Unless Mr. Wender decides to have a pop quiz."

"Which he usually does," Rose says.

"Exactly."

We watch as the bus turns the corner, and then it stops in front of us. The doors open, and we walk up the steps and take a seat in the middle. Leon and Graham are there, but they're all the way in the back and aren't allowed to get out of their seats.

I pull out my phone and put in one of my earphones, and Rose takes the other one.

"This song?" she says. "I thought you got over this one."

"Just because I have a new number one favorite song," I say, "doesn't mean I stopped loving this one."

She shrugs, and I leave the song on.

We get to the school three songs later, and we pile out of the bus and walk into prison.

I mean school.

No, I really don't.

Rose and I go our separate ways, each of us heading to our own lockers. I put in the combination for mine and open it to put my backpack away and get my books.

"Hey."

I jump and turn to my right, where Leon is standing, holding his backpack. "Did I scare you?" he asks, trying not to laugh.

"No," I say. "Yes. Maybe a little."

He chuckles. "So are we still going to hang out after you're finished working?"

"Who said I was going in the first place?" I say.

"Because if you don't, I'll stay there the whole night waiting," he says.

"No, you won't," I say.

"If you don't show up," he says. "I will." He holds out his pinky. "And that's a promise."

I look at his hand, and then up at him. "Really?"

"Really."

"Seriously?"

"Seriously."

I sigh. "You're weird, you know that?"

"Thank you."

I roll my eyes and interlock my pinky with his.

"And a pinky promise is legit," he says. "If someone breaks a pinky promise, you can never trust that person again."

"Leon, promises are kind of made to be broken," I say. "Literally. If someone makes a promise, at least one of them is always thinking, 'They're going to break it, they don't mean it.' They never think, 'Wow, this person is amazing for going through with the promise.'"

"That, Marissa Anne, is because there's no more trust in this world. That's not the type of world that God created," he says.

"No one really gives us a good reason to have any trust," I say, putting my hand back down.

He smiles and puts his hand down also. "Then let's give them one," he says. "I promise that if you don't go tonight, I will stay there all night. I have to go. I'll see you later."

And he walks away before I can say anything.

CHAPTER FIVE

"Okay, name at least fifty elements of the periodic table."

"Fifty?" I say, and Graham nods. "Is this all going to be on the test?"

"Actually, on the test you have to name all of them," he says. "I'm going easy on you right now."

I groan and put my head down on the table. "So should I be *thanking* you?"

"Yeah, kind of," he says.

I sit up and glare at him. "That was *sarcasm.*"

"I know," he says. "It's your most fluent language."

"Shut up," I say.

"Are you going to name them, or not?" he asks.

"Off the top of my head?" I ask.

"The test isn't going to be an open book, so yes, off the top of your head," he says.

"Um, let me think …" I mutter. "Boron, Carbon, Hydrogen, Helium, Neon, Carbon, Iron, Gold, Silver, Lithium, Beryllium, Nitrogen, Oxygen, Fluorine… can I write it down? I think better when I'm writing."

He passes me a piece of paper and pencil. "Go ahead."

I write down as many as I can think of without numbering or counting them, and when I think I have enough, I put down the pencil and hand it back to him. He reads them over quietly, then says, "Marissa, you wrote down fifty-three."

"I did?"

"Yes, you did," he says. "I'm surprised, considering how much you procrastinate."

"Hey!" I say, but then calm down. "Honestly, I'm surprised at myself, too."

"See? I'm not the only one!" he says.

"Either way, you're annoying."

"If genius is considered annoying to you, then yes, I'm annoying."

I roll my eyes and gather my stuff. "At least you finally admitted it."

Ignoring my remark, he puts his books away and says, "So, I guess I'll see you later."

"No, I don't think I'm going," I say.

"Are you kidding me?" he says. "If you don't go, Leon said he'd sleep in that parking lot."

"I doubt it," I say.

"Suit yourself," Graham says and heads out the doors. "But I still think you're going."

"What makes you say that?" I call after him, but he doesn't answer.

Why does he always have to do that? Leaving me in suspense, even more curious than before.

"It's easy to torture a curious person."

Whether Leon would actually sleep in that parking lot or not, I don't know. Because, in the end, Graham is right.

I go to the parking lot.

I'm sitting in Rose's bedroom, holding a scrap of paper in one hand and my phone in the other. I keep glancing at both of them. Phone, paper, phone, paper, phone, paper. I'm sleeping at Rose's house again because, not surprisingly, my mom has to work late. Except this time, she's taking an overnight shift. At least today I got a fair warning so I'm prepared. In the scrap of paper I hold in my hand, it has two numbers. The ones Graham gave me three whole months ago, that I have not called until now. That just proves how much I procrastinate.

I need to call Graham to ask him what chapter I'm supposed to be studying (sure I pay attention, but not that much), but he still hasn't told me which number is his. So whichever one I call, it could end up being Leon.

"Marissa!" Rose says, snapping me out of my daze.

"Huh?" I say.

"Why does it matter?" she says. "Either way, you'll end up either talking to your tutor and get answers, or your crush," she shrugs. "It's a win-win situation."

"First, he is *not* my crush," I say. "Second, it would just be awkward."

"How?"

"I—" I was hoping she wouldn't ask that question, but now that she has, I have no idea how to respond. "It just would, okay?"

"Okay, whatever," she says. "How about this: I'll dial in the number, but then you have to take the phone when they answer."

"That makes absolutely no difference!" I say.

"Technically, it does," she says.

"No, because in the end, I still have to *talk!*"

"Deal with it."

She reaches over and snatches my phone from my hands and the paper from the other.

"Now, to call," she says.

"Now for me to meet my doom," I correct and lay down face first on her bed, using two pillows to cover my ears and eyes.

"Oh, stop being so overdramatic." Rose puts the phone up to her ear as the phone rings.

All of a sudden, she pulls the pillow away from me and gives me the phone.

"Talk!" she whisper-shouts.

"Fine," I say and take the phone. "Hello?"

"Marissa?" I hear a voice on the other end of the line.

"Yeah, who is this?" I ask.

"It's Leon."

Of course.

"Oh, sorry I meant to call Graham," I say, hoping I don't sound rude. "Because I need him to help with my homework, so ..."

"Oh ..." he mutters. "Well, do you think that maybe I can text you later? Not now, obviously, since you're going to call Graham."

"Sure," I say. "See you tomorrow."

"Bye."

"Bye."

I hang up and turn to Rose. "Wrong number?" she asks.

"It was Leon."

"Ooh ..." she says. "Now that I think of it, it is awkward."

"At least now I know that the other one is Graham's," I shrug.

"Then call it," she replies, picking up a magazine and leaning back on the pile of pillows.

I take the piece of paper with the number and put it in.

It rings once. Twice. Three times.

"Hello?"

"Graham?" I ask.

"No, it's Leon. Marissa?"

"Yeah. Is this Graham's phone?" I ask.

"No, it's my house phone," he says.

"Was the number I called before Graham's phone?"

"No, I would've told you," I can sense him smiling through the phone. "The numbers he gave you—were they both mine?"

"Apparently," I mumble. "I'm going to kill him."

"It was God's doing, let's say."

"It was *Graham*, Leon, shut up."

He laughs. "Rose is there, isn't she?"

"Yep."

"Then she can help you," he says. "Isn't she like, a straight-A student?"

"Of course," I say.

"There you go, then," he says. "So, do you think that we can meet up after school tomorrow?"

"In the parking lot?"

"No, maybe we can go somewhere else this time," he says. "Adventures aren't made in only *one* place."

"But a lot of them are," I reply.

"But we've been there … how many times now?"

"Lost count."

"See, losing count means an infinite amount," he says. "That's a lot."

"That's true," I agree. "Fine, we'll go somewhere else tomorrow. But where?"

"We'll figure it out," he says.

"We always do," I say. "There's always some place for some immature idiots to hang out."

He laughs again.

"I'm not that funny, don't laugh," I say.

"Shut up, I laughed because you're funny *and* because I agree," he says.

"Whatever," I say. "You're weird, Graeme."

"Thank you," he says. "And that's not the first time you've said that."

"I know," I reply. "And that's not the first time you thanked me for saying it."

We're both quiet for a minute, me, smiling like a dork, and I can only imagine whatever he's doing.

"I'll see you tomorrow," I say breaking the silence.

"See you," he says. "Oh, and Marissa?"

"Yeah?"

"Try not to beat yourself up over schoolwork or anything like that," he says. "School is important, but don't stress too much about it."

"Thanks."

I hang up the phone and lay back down on the bed.

"Hmmm …" Rose mutters, without looking up from her magazine.

"What?" I ask.

"Oh, nothing," she says. "Just that smile on your face."

I didn't even notice that I was still smiling. That's weird. I try to stop, but I can't. I turn over and lay on my stomach.

"What about it?"

"I know that smile," she says. "You like him."

"Of course," I say. "You have to like a friend for them to *be* a friend."

She shakes her head. "No, you like him as *more* than just a friend."

"No, I don't."

"Yes, you do."

"No, I *don't.*"

"Yes, you *do.*"

"No, I don't!"

"Look, I get it if you're afraid to admit it," Rose says. "But he obviously feels the same way. Don't screw this up."

I roll my eyes and pick up a magazine. "I don't, okay? If you'll excuse me, I want to read my horoscope."

She laughs and lies down next to me. "I thought you didn't believe in this kind of stuff!"

"And you're right," I say. "I think that it's a waste of time, but I really don't care. I read it to make fun of it."

"What's your star sign?" she asks.

"Don't you know when my birthday is?" I reply.

"Of course, I do," she says. "But I don't know which star sign is for what."

"Neither do I," I admit and then look over at the magazine. "I am a … Capricorn."

"Huh," she mutters. "And what am I?"

"You're a …" I search for it on the magazine page. "Libra."

"Libra," she repeats. "Kind of sounds like library."

"Maybe that's because it's in the word library," I say sarcastically.

"Shut up."

"Okay."

"What does your horoscope say?" she asks.

"You told me to shut up," I say.

"Figure of speech," she says quickly. "What does it say?"

"Yours says," I say, "'*you can spot the tiniest details out of place today.*'"

"The irony," she mutters.

"And mine says," my eyes quickly scan over it, and then I read it out loud. "'*You may need a translator to get through to people today.*'"

"Huh," Rose mumbles. "And this was for today?"

"No, actually it's for tomorrow," I answer. "So you got to keep an eye out, and I need a translator."

"But who could be your translator?" Rose says. "I'm horrible at reading emotions."

"Yet you think that Leon likes me," I say.

"That's different," she says. "It's obvious!"

"Not even," I say. "He's like, popular!"

"What's your point?" she says.

"That my only friends are you, Graham, and him. Which gives me another reason," I say. "Making up rumors ruins friendships."

"What if it's not just a rumor?"

"Then that'll make it even worse," I say. "And it's a rumor. Which *you're* making!"

"Hey, you're the only person I talk to about this!" she says. "And Graham a little bit, but that's not the point."

I climb up to the pillows and go under the covers. "I'm just going to ignore you and sleep."

"You can ignore me all you want," she says, as she gets ready for bed. "But you can't ignore the butterflies."

"I thought you said you would text me yesterday."

I grab my books and turn to Leon, leaning against the locker next to mine.

"No, *you* said that you would text *me,*" I correct. "Which you didn't."

"How was I supposed to know when you were done with your homework?" he says.

"It doesn't really matter," I say.

"It kind of does?"

"Why?"

"Because I wanted to talk to you!"

"You talk to me at school!" I say, raising my voice. I want to get upset at him, but the situation is too funny, and I'm smiling. "And we hang out after school too."

"So?" he asks.

"*So,* isn't that enough?" I ask.

He pauses and thinks for a second. "Nope."

"You know, most people would want to *stop* talking and avoid me," I say.

"Those people don't know what they're missing," he says, and I hope that I stop myself in time from blushing. "It's a *privilege* to talk to you. And hey, remember, that phone call was God's doing."

"Shut up and get some sanity," I say.

"Sucks for the people who listen to that," he says. "The more insane you are, the better."

"Yeah, yeah."

I rummage through my locker, and he's quiet for a second, just staring at me.

"Have you been eating?"

I did *not* see that coming.

"Why do you ask?" I say, slowly turning to him.

"Why don't you answer?" he says.

I sigh. "What do you think?" I turn back to my locker.

"Marissa, this is serious stuff," he says. "This isn't good for you! You're already so skinny and pale, you can't get it to be any worse!"

I ignore him.

"Marissa," he says. "Marissa, look at me."

He grabs my shoulder and spins me to face him, and I shove his hand away.

"No, I haven't been eating, okay?" I say. He's upset, it's obvious, but so am I. "And really, it's none of your concern."

"I'm worried about you," he says. "I don't want anything bad to happen to you."

"It's a bit too late for that," I say. "Bad things started happening to me a while ago. By now I've gotten used to it."

"What bad things?" he asks.

"*People* are bad," I say. "And sadly, they're all around us."

"Who?" he asks.

"I'm not just going to point them out!" I say. "Besides, most of them are dead or have left me!"

A look of concern flashes across his face. Or it's pity. I don't need him to feel bad for me. I'm fine.

I slam my locker shut.

"Why do you have to make everything so difficult?" he says quietly, not meeting my eyes.

"This isn't the first time you've asked me that, and my answer is still the same," I explain. "I'm not trying to, but I have my walls up for a reason."

"What's that reason then?" he asks.

"I trust no one," I say. "Only the people who I *know* I can, who have been put through the same things I have and have stuck with me through enough that I know that they don't just abandon me in the worst situations."

"Who do you trust?"

"Rose and my mom and …" I pause, hesitant. "That's it."

"Do you trust me?"

I look down at the ground. Why did he have to ask that?

"No, I don't," I say. "I can't." The bell rings. "I can't hang out after school today. I'll see you tomorrow."

I walk away before he can say another word.

I walk into my house and drop my bag by the door.

"Hi Marissa," my mom says. She's making something. Probably bread.

"Hey, Mom." I lean against the counter. "Whatcha making?"

"Bread," she says.

I knew it.

"It's a different kind this time," she says.

"What do you mean?" I ask.

"Cinnamon bread," she explains, beating the dough. "I put cinnamon in it, and when it's done, sprinkle some on top."

"Sounds good," I say.

"I hope so," she says. "I found the recipe online."

I laugh. My mom is always trying some new recipe that she finds. Surprisingly enough, most of them turn out pretty good. Unlike the foreign rice that somehow managed to get stuck on the walls. Don't even ask me how she did that one; I still wonder about it to this day.

"How did you learn how to make bread in the first place? Like, regular bread," I ask. "Online again?"

"It was a long time ago," she says, still working the dough. "And no, it was not online," she glances at me and then looks back. "Your father taught me."

I freeze. Everything in my body is screaming, *Uncharted territory! Abort question!*

But, of course, I can't take back words. I have to continue with the conversation, hoping that maybe it'll get better. But a part of me actually wants to talk about this. Wants to talk about him.

Thankfully, I don't have to say anything because she continues talking. "When we first married," she says, "we didn't have any money. Sure, we had jobs, but they didn't pay very well. We lived in a very small house and could barely afford the rent each month. And back then, the ingredients for bread cost less than a loaf of bread itself. So I would buy the ingredients, and we would make bread to eat. And when we wanted something sweet, all I could do was roll the bread in sugar."

I don't say anything for a second, busy thinking all of this over. "How did you manage to get by?" I ask.

"Laughter," she says.

"What?" I say. "How does laughter help in any way?"

She picks up the dough and puts it in the pan she's using. "If you have someone who makes you laugh in the toughest times, who can always make you smile *no matter what*, even if you have nothing," she smiles, "then you have everything."

She opens the oven, puts the bread in, sets a timer and heads to the sink to wash her hands. "We would actually *joke* about our state. We would talk about how someday we would live in a big old house with enough money to get by, and even more. We were happy because we had each other."

She turns off the sink, and I can't help but ask, "Do you miss him?"

She sighs and turns to me as she dries her hands. "Of course," she says. "But we'll see him again someday."

"How?"

She smiles, walks towards me and pulls me into a hug.

"In heaven," she says. "Right now, he's just taking a long nap."

"Can dead people dream?" I ask pulling away like a curious child.

"No," she says. "It's like the blink of an eye. Except when you open your eyes again, you will see angels. And they will be singing."

"That sounds a bit out there, don't you think?" I say.

"I guess it does," she says. "But I have been reading the Bible, and that's what it says. I believe it. It's my hope. And you should believe it too."

I nod slowly. I desperately need to believe it.

"I want to see him again, Mom. I really do." She kisses my forehead. "We will sweetheart. We will." Then I turn to pick up my backpack and go upstairs to my room.

As I go to the staircase, I hear my mom call, "Marissa?"

I look over. "Yeah, Mom?"

"Make sure you're with someone who makes you smile," she says. "If they do the opposite, then they're really not worth it."

I nod again and then head upstairs, where I'm alone with my thoughts.

CHAPTER SIX

"What's something that you really want to do?" Leon asks a week later. "Like, that's simple."

We're walking around the park near my house, and I'm holding my skateboard. We hadn't planned to meet up here. He just saw me walking in this direction, and since Rose and Graham are both somewhere today, he followed.

I think for a second. "That's simple?"

"Yeah," he says. "And inexpensive."

I laugh. "So I guess Disney World is out of the question."

"How in the world is Disney World simple or inexpensive?"

I ignore him. "Hmm … something simple and inexpensive …"

I'm quiet for two seconds more, but apparently that's too long for him.

"Is this really so hard?" he says.

"No, it's really not," I say. "And I'm sure that I can think of something if you can shut up for ten seconds."

"Okay," he says. "I'll keep count."

"Don't count out loud, I'll get distracted."

"You're very picky,"

"Just *shhh*," I shush. "Ten seconds, go."

I roll my eyes and then start thinking of something.

"Three, two, one," Leon mutters. "Time's up! You think of anything?"

"Yes, but one question first," I say. "Why do you want to know?"

He shrugs. "Just to know."

"Well," I say. "You know that thing above highways? Not the one for cars, the one where there's either a ramp or a staircase leading up to it, and you can look down at the highway, and there's like, a cage around it?"

"I think I do," he says.

"For some strange reason, I've always wanted to go up there," I explain. "Never got the chance to, though."

"What's something that *you've* always wanted to do?" I ask. "That's simple and inexpensive?"

"Does bungee-jumping count?" he says immediately.

"You judge me for saying Disney World," I say. "And then suggest bungee-jumping?"

"Okay, so maybe it's not simple …"

"Obviously," I interrupt.

"But there are some places where it's inexpensive!"

"Oh, yeah?" I say. "Name one."

"Um …" he hesitates.

"See? You can't think of anything."

"I would have to Google it!"

I roll my eyes. "Seriously, Leon. Is it that hard to think of something?"

"Okay, I've always wanted to jump off a waterfall," he says. "And there's this place that I used to go to when I was a kid, and I had the chance to do it, but I chickened out. I regret it completely now, though."

"So that's why you want to do it?" I ask. "Because you were a wimp?"

"I was not—"

I cut him off with a glare.

"Maybe I was," he admits. "But that's not the main reason. Even back then, I wanted to do it because I thought that it would feel like flying. That's *still* the reason I want to do it. Because I think it'll be like flying. Same for bungee-jumping and skydiving."

"But it's not really flying, is it? You're just … falling."

"I can't think of falling without flying," he says.

"And I can't think of flying without falling," I say.

"That's because I'm an optimist—besides that, I believe in angels—and you're a pessimist."

"I am not a pessimist!" I say. "I'm a realist. Big difference."

"Yeah, because reality is *so* great," he says.

"It can be," I say, and then scoff. "Now *I* sound like an optimist, and *you* sound like a pessimist."

"I'm just saying that pessimists and realists are pretty much the same thing," he says, and then looks at me, and my blank stare. "You don't get it, do you? Do I need to explain it?"

"No, I actually get it," I say. "It's not hard to understand."

"For others it is."

"That's because they're simple-minded, and we're such intellectuals," I say sarcastically.

He laughs harshly. "We're opposites, yet you get me. How is that possible?"

"I don't know," I say. "It just *is*."

Leon turns and walks past me towards this huge willow tree, lies down under it, and closes his eyes.

"What are you doing?" I ask.

He opens his eyes and sits up, leaning on his elbows. "I'm relaxing," he pats the spot next to him. "Come here."

I hesitantly walk over and sit down next to him. "Why is this so relaxing?" I ask.

"How is it *not?*" he says and lies back down, but keeps his eyes open. He points up to the sky. "See the clouds?"

I look up and roll my eyes. "Uh, yes?"

"You sounded unsure," he says. I lie down next to him and stare at the sky.

Ignoring him, I ask, "Anyway, what is it about the clouds?"

"Can't you see some shapes in them?" he says.

"I see blobs," I answer. "And cotton candy."

"Does cotton candy even have a shape?" he asks.

"No, which proves my point."

He laughs, a shy, small laugh, unlike when he's laughing so much he can't control it, and even though I love both of them, I mostly like when he's louder and doesn't care who hears him.

"How about that one?" he says, pointing at the biggest cloud in the sky. "It kind of looks like a dragon."

For people with small or no imagination, it would look like just another cloud, but that's not what we see. Maybe that's why I like being around him, besides the fact that he makes me happy. Because he's just as crazy as I am.

"It does," I agree. "But it's transforming."

"Now it looks like …" I don't let him finish.

"A dragon using his fire-breathing powers against a knight holding a sword and a pig," I say.

"Where do you see a pig?"

"Right there. The little squiggly cloud is the tail."

"Oh, I see it now!"

He looks over at me and smiles, and I look over at him and smile back, and we stay like that awhile, and I think about what color his eyes really are. Hazel? Or blue? They seem to shine against the dark blue shirt he's wearing, but I can't be sure. But then his eyes flicker away and the moment is broken.

"So," I say, trying to make it less awkward. "Do you believe God made the clouds too?"

"Duh," he says. "Who else could've made them?"

I shrug. "I don't know. I guess I was never really so sure about that kind of stuff."

"But you used to be, right?"

My eyes widen, and I glance at him. "How would you know that?" I ask.

He laughed. "You kind of said it at the parking lot."

I look back at the sky. "I have my reasons," I say.

He doesn't push anymore, much to my luck, but then he asks, "So what *do* you believe in?"

"I dunno."

"God?"

"Maybe." "Angels?"

"Kind of."

"Guardian angels?"

"No."

"Why not?" he asks.

"Because if there are guardian angels, then where's mine?" I retort. "And why hasn't he protected my dad from death?"

"But you don't believe anymore."

"Yeah, but I used to," I say. "And the so-called 'guardian angels' didn't protect my dad. He also let me go through some harsh moments in the past!"

Leon shrugs. "God lets things happen for a reason, you know?" he says. "Whatever you're not telling me, whatever you went through, it was all for a reason, it was all for the best. I promise you that."

When I don't respond, he continues.

"Anyway, how about an afterlife?" he asks.

"I don't know. I mean, I believe in *something* after death, but I don't know if I believe in heaven or hell or purgatory."

"I don't believe in purgatory," he says. "But I do believe in heaven."

"Not hell?"

"Nope."

"Why not?"

"*For the wages of sin is death, but the gift of God is eternal life*," he says. When hc sees how confused I am, he continues explaining. "It's Romans 6:23, and it's basically saying that God doesn't want us to be punished eternally. He wants us to live eternally. But if we sin, then—" he shrugs. "The wages of sin is death."

"You believe that?"

"One hundred percent," he grins.

"So, God really does love everyone?"

He tilts his head and looks at me with curiosity and confusion. "Why wouldn't you believe that?"

I don't really want to talk about that and try to find an escape route. I check my phone for the time and then raise my eyebrow.

"Well," I say, sitting up. "I should get home."

He stands up and offers me his hand to help me up, and I take it.

"You've never been to my house, have you?" he asks.

"No, I haven't," I say, already walking back the way we came. "Why?"

He walks faster to catch up to me. "Because I've been to your house."

"Did you?"

"Don't you remember?" he says. "When Graham, Rose and I went over a while ago on a Sunday morning and just hung out playing video games? We played *Mario Kart* and some game that you used to love as a kid."

"*Little Big Planet,*" I say.

"Yes, that's it!" he says.

"Yeah, I remember. But it's weird that you remember all that in detail."

"It's weird that you *don't*."

"Whatever," I say. "Again, why does it matter?"

"Since I've already seen your house," he says, "I want you to see mine."

"No."

"Why not?" he whines.

"Why should I?" I mimic him.

"Because I want you to," he says. "Please?"

I sigh. "Why do you want me to?" "You ask 'why' far too much."

"So do you!"

"I'm just an idiot who asks random stuff."

"I'm very much aware, thank you."

He ignores me. "Come on. Just this once."

"You don't mean that," I say.

"Maybe, maybe not," he says. "So?"

I roll my eyes. "Fine. Just this once."

"Great, now let's go." He grabs my hand and pulls me after him. He has that big smile on his face that makes him seem like an eager and overly excited little kid going to a circus.

"I still don't understand why this is so important to you," I say.

"See, now you're using that word again," he says.

"What word?"

"'*Why*.'"

"But I don't overuse it!"

"Your words, not mine."

"Hey!"

"Okay, we'll talk about this at my house," he says. "But for now, save your breath because we're going to run."

"What?"

And then we're both running with my pulse racing, and he's dragging me after him, with his hand in mine. I'm laughing, and so is he, yet at the same time, we're both trying to catch our breath, even though that's obviously not working.

We cover the path we walked on so much faster than we did before, and I have to admit, I don't even remember the last time I ran this fast. And then black spots begin to cloud my vision, and I panic. I've passed out many times in my bedroom while doing simple tasks. But I can't make Leon suspect anything. He already knows that I'm anorexic. I have to go through with this and pretend that nothing's happening.

Thankfully, we arrive at his house and it's over. We're still laughing breathlessly outside his house, trying to get air into our lungs and trying to slow our heart rate down. The blackness fades away, and I calm down.

"You okay?" he asks when he can finally talk.

I nod. "Yeah. Yeah, I'm fine."

"Okay, good." He straightens up. "Let's go inside."

He walks up the porch steps and stands beside the door. "You coming?"

I follow him, and he opens the door for me and makes a motion. "After you."

I laugh. "No need to be proper."

"I'm not!" he protests.

"Sure," I say sarcastically.

"Just go inside," he says impatiently.

"No need to be pushy, either."

I step inside and can already see that Leon's family has really good taste in decor. I'm also relieved that I was smart enough to leave my skateboard outside. There are a *lot* of those little pictures and frames on the walls, and a white sofa (a freaking WHITE SOFA) with some black throw pillows on it. I'm surprised that they trust him with that, since every time he buys himself ice cream or he's eating something, he drops at least some of it.

"I know what you're thinking," he says. "And I'm not allowed to eat or play video games there."

"I knew it."

He laughs, and then a tall woman comes into the room. I notice that she has the same big smile that Leon has, so I figure she's obviously his mother.

"Hi, Leon," she says. "Who's this?"

She walks over to us, and I suddenly feel self-conscious. What if she doesn't like me? What if his dad doesn't like me? What if I do something stupid or clumsy and she comes to the realization that I really *am* stupid and clumsy? Why am I freaking out? It's not like we're dating!

Thankfully, Leon saves me.

"Oh, this is Marissa," he says. "I just wanted to show her around."

I stick out my hand, and she shakes it.

"So this is the famous Marissa?" she says.

"Famous?" I ask, glancing at Leon.

"Mom …" Leon says in a warning voice.

"I've heard a lot about you," she says.

"Oh, you have?" I raise my eyebrows at him.

"I have to say he's right," she adds.

"About what?"

"You do seem like a rare person."

"Mom …" he says again.

"Sorry?" I ask.

"Well, most people don't leave that much of an impression on him," she says. "Most of the time, he's talking about how much he loved a person's smile from that game he and Graham play, but there's always something that he has to say about you. Good things, of course. It's mostly about how—"

"MOM!" Leon says, shaking his head quickly, and when he catches me looking at him, he plasters on a fake smile and pretends that he wasn't doing anything.

His mom gives what I translate into that evil smile that only a mother gives when she knows something you don't, and I decide that I like Mrs. Graeme.

"I'll just leave you two," she says. "Leon, you can show her around, and then take her to the den if she wants."

"Thank you!" I say as she walks away and through another door.

I turn to Leon, and there's this awkward silence for a minute as we just stand there, both of us staring down at our feet. I look up at him, and that's when I realize how tall he is. My forehead reaches a bit under the bridge of his nose, and since I'm short and about 5'3 and a half (the half always counts), he must be about 5'8 or something. He's still looking at the carpet though as if admiring the maroon pattern of diamonds and triangles on it.

I finally decide to break the silence. "She seems pretty cool."

"She is," he says. "Though there are times she can be a bit embarrassing."

I smile. "How do you know that's not why I think she's cool?"

His eyes finally look up to meet mine. "Is it?"

"Maybe," I say. "Maybe not."

"What's that supposed to mean?" he asks.

"Wouldn't you like to know?" I reply.

"Yeah, I actually would!" he says.

"You will," I say. "Eventually."

"I'm just going to ignore your sarcasm and sass—"

I cut him off. "You can't ignore either of those things if at least one of them is in every sentence."

"Which one was in that sentence?" he asks.

"Sass," I say as if it's the most obvious thing in the world.

"Well, I'm just going to *try* to ignore that," he corrects himself. "While I show you around. How's that?"

"Works for me."

He smiles at me, and it's not the half-smile from before or the fake one he just had; it's that full-out, huge smile that I love.

Leon walks off and motions for me to go with him, so I do, and we fall into step. He turns a corner and leads me up a long winding staircase, with designs on the railing.

He sees my reaction and says, "Yeah, I know. Fancy, right? Came with the house."

"Can you even tell what they are?" I ask, and thankfully he knows that I'm talking about the designs carved in.

"They're vines with apples hanging from them," he says. "It looks nice."

"What is with apples?" I ask when we reach the top of the staircase. "They're so popular. Don't the other fruits feel left out?"

"Probably because of fairytales," he says. "You know, the poisoned apple? Or the Bible story of Adam and Eve."

We reach the end of the staircase but stay standing there. "But why is it the apple?" I ask. "Why can't it be like, a peach or something?"

"When we first had a real conversation at lunch this year, you were eating an apple," he points out.

"You remember that?" I say.

"Duh," he says. "Why is it that I remember everything and you don't?"

"Bad memory?" I suggest. "It's the only thing I can think of."

"I remember a lot of things," he says.

"I bet you even remember being born," I joke.

"Yes, I remember coming into the world and the doctor saying, 'You're going to regret this, kid.' Now can we go?"

I laugh and say, "Sure, fine."

We walk down this hallway with beige walls and family pictures that have quotes surrounding the frame like, 'Live well, Love much, Laugh often'. He turns and heads into a room, which I figure is his, judging by the posters and PlayStation, but he surprises me.

"This is my little brother's room," he says. "He's about six turning seven, so he doesn't get half the stuff we talk about and can't play any video games besides Mario, Sonic, and Pokémon."

"Ah, makes sense."

"Yep," he agrees. "Now I'll show you my room."

He walks out and heads into the room across the hall. When he opens the door, I immediately think that I should've known that Leon would have this kind of room and not the other one. On the posters in the other room, it had video game characters and some cheesy quotes that would be found on graphic T-shirts for ten-year-olds, the ones that say, 'You can't spell awesome without ME,' and the wallpaper had little aliens all over it. I can't believe I didn't pay attention or notice any of that until I walked in here.

His room has pale blue walls, and his bedspread is green. He has a TV, of course, and an Xbox, and a desk with a laptop, where the screensaver is a picture of him and Graham.

"Are you guys jumping ...?"

"Off a cliff?" he grins proudly. "Yeah. It was at this water park, where they had this attraction. But it was the kind of 'Do At Your Own Risk' thing, so he broke his leg."

"So you can jump off a cliff, but not a waterfall?"

"It was at a water park!"

I smile to myself and continue looking around. There's a bookshelf, and I recognize almost all the books there, and another shelf with CDs. He doesn't have many posters, just two or three, and they're all of bands. Besides that, he just has some pictures hanging on the walls taken from a Polaroid camera, and I recognize some, like the one of us and Graham and Rose laughing at a carnival. My head is thrown back in the picture, and my mouth is open laughing, and a part of me realizes how much clothes I'm wearing in the picture while they're wearing shorts and T-shirts. I quickly push the thought away.

"You seem surprised," Leon says.

I look at him and shrug. "Not really, actually. This was kind of expected."

"Am I really that predictable?" he asks.

"Sort of, yes," I say.

"How so?"

"This just seems so ..." I search for the right word but can't find it. "You, I guess. It seems like everything you would do, and everything you talk about. Especially the bands on the posters."

"Those are old bands," he says.

"I know. I mean," I point to one of them, "The Rolling Stones? You like original music. I know that."

"Do I really mention music that often?" he asks, laughter in his eyes.

"No," I say. "But you mention it enough for me to know which ones you like and which ones you can't stand."

"Name a band or singer I can't stand," he challenges.

"Any sappy romantic singer or rappers that make the next stupid thing."

"Name a *stupid thing* or catchphrase I can't stand."

"You hate the word 'swag' and you don't like snapbacks."

"You really do know me."

"I know."

He pauses. "Do you want to stay longer, or can I walk you home now?"

I think it over. "Could we play video games?" I ask slowly.

"Of course," he says.

I follow him back through the hallway and down the staircase, and then through another hall that opens into a wide area with a flat-screen TV, a black leather sofa, and beanbags.

He turns on the Xbox, puts in a random game, and passes me a controller.

"You are going to sit on the sofa?" he asks.

"Sofas are for losers," I joke, and throw myself onto a blue beanbag.

"You're pretty predictable too," he says as he sits on a red one.

"What do you mean?"

"Most people would want the sofa and jump on it first chance they get," he explains to me. "While you chose the beanbag, no hesitation."

"What's wrong with that?" I question.

"Nothing," he says. "I just think that you're different."

"In a good way?"

"I don't see any other way."

The game turns on, and he hits play and the game begins. When we're picking characters, I turn to the toughest guy I can get with a small weapon, which leaves him stuck with the girl in the game carrying a dagger, and that just proves that he always lets me get the first choice and is happy with whatever is leftover, and I'm thankful for someone like that, who can show me that you can be happy with the smallest things in life that no one wants.

We crawl through a cave that kind of looks like the one from *Batman,* and we fight some sort of zombie that can't scare anybody.

"The graphics really aren't that good," Leon says.

"I honestly don't care," I say.

"But the game is also lame," he says.

"I still don't care," I repeat. "Do you?"

"No," he says. "I'm just seeing if you care."

"Now you know I don't."

"Most people would."

I glance at him. "I thought we already clarified that I'm not like most people."

He nods. "Good point."

At that moment, we hear the front door slam and footsteps coming in our direction. I glance over and emerging from the hallway is a little boy with scruffy brown hair and bright blue eyes, holding a bicycle helmet.

"Leon!" The boy squeals.

"Hey, squirt," Leon smiles, quickly pausing the game.

'Squirt' runs over to Leon, gives him a quick hug, and turns to me.

"Who's she?" he asks pointing to me.

"I want you to meet Marissa," Leon says to him. "And Marissa, this is my little brother, Xander."

The little boy waves at me. "Hi, Marissa!" he says, and I wave back.

"Hey, what're you doing home early?" Leon asks him.

"Graham brought me," Xander says.

"Is he here?"

He nods, just as we hear another set of footsteps getting closer, and Graham comes out.

"Hey, Leon," he says. "Xander, your mom's calling you."

Xander quickly runs out of the room and Graham walks over and finally notices me.

"Marissa?" he says, shocked.

I give a small wave. "Hey, Graham."

"How come I wasn't invited to this?" he asks.

Here we go. Graham being overdramatic. I warned Leon that he shouldn't have taken acting because it would get to his head, but did he listen?

Absolutely not.

"Dude, it wasn't even planned," Leon says.

"Yeah," I agree, backing him up. "We just bumped into each other, walked around at the park and then he wanted me to see his house since I've never been here."

"In the time that you two have known each other, living just a few steps away," Graham says. "You never went to his house?"

"Never really cared to," I say.

"Hey!" Leon looks at me.

"How is that offensive?" I ask.

"How is it not?" he retorts, but I could tell that he's suppressing a laugh.

"All I'm saying is that I didn't really care if I came or not."

"But that's offensive to my home!"

"Okay, sorry," I grab another controller. "Here, Graham, take this, and we'll add you to the game."

"Oh, and you think that that's just going to make it all better?" Graham snaps, but I can tell that he's trying not to laugh, so I shrug and put the extra control down.

"Suit yourself," I mutter.

Graham pauses, and then says, "You know my weakness," and proceeds to walk over, picks up the remote, and settles down in the green beanbag.

I laugh as Leon presses play in the game and Graham joins. I'm sitting right in between them so I can talk to them both without having to look across someone.

"Hey, Marissa?" Leon says.

"Yes, Leon?"

He looks at me. "Do you trust me now?"

"Not really because I almost died since you're not paying attention," I smile. "By the way, a zombie's about to kill you."

He turns his attention back to the game and keeps playing, quickly dodging the zombie. "But seriously, do you?" he asks.

"You guys are still going on about this?" Graham interrupts.

"Man, I just want to know if she trusts me," Leon says to him.

"Is it *that hard* to trust him?" Graham turns to me. "Because you trust me, so…"

"Oh, really?" Leon says, raising his eyebrows at me.

"Nice job, Graham," I mumble.

"I was just trying to help!" he protests.

"And how did that work out?"

"How come you trust *him* and not *me?*" Leon asks.

"Because I've talked to him longer and more than you," I explain.

"That doesn't mean anything."

"*And,*" I say. "He's my tutor. And he's pretty good at it. I have to trust him so he can teach me. If he were a jerk, he would've given me wrong answers. So far, he hasn't failed me yet."

Leon's quiet. "How much do you trust me?" he asks.

"Why can't you just play the game?" I ask.

"Oh, you said it again."

"Huh?"

"You said *why.*"

"What?" Graham says.

"Doesn't she ask *why* a lot?" Leon asks him.

"Because she wonders a lot," Graham explains. "I thought you knew that by now!"

"Thank you, Graham!" I say and then turn to Leon. "See, *that's* why I trust him more."

"You're very welcome, Marissa," Graham says smiling, pleased that he can be of *some* use.

"Really, how much do you trust me?" Leon asks again.

"Am I the only one concentrating on the game?" Graham asks.

"Shut up," Leon says to him, and then turns back to me. "Marissa?"

"Hmm ..." I mutter.

"And?"

"Fifty-fifty," I tell him.

Leon looks back at the game. "It's better than before."

"How much was it before?" Graham says.

Leon pauses, hesitant to answer. "Zero," he mutters.

Graham shrugs and leans forward to focus once again on the game. "It's an improvement."

The phone rings once. And then twice. And when I'm about to give up, she answers.

"I know, I'm late, I'm sorry, but I'm almost there," she says immediately.

"Rose, we're all waiting for you," I say into the phone. "Graham and Leon are already here. And they also brought Xander, and he's getting restless."

"Don't blame me," Graham says pointing at Leon. "The cotton candy was his idea."

"I didn't think he would get like this!" Leon defends himself.

"Oh, gee, you didn't think giving sugar to a little kid would make him hyperactive?" Graham says sarcastically. "Who would've known?"

"Shut up!" I tell them both and then turn back to Rose on the phone. "How far are you?"

"Be there in five …" she counts. "Four …"

"Rose, saying it doesn't make it true."

"Three …"

"Rose."

"Two … turn around."

I turn and standing behind me is Rose.

"I told you," she says as she puts her phone away. "Now let's go because I didn't save up money for nothing."

We're at an actual amusement park, not a carnival or festival, a legit amusement park where tickets cost more than twenty bucks each, for the first time in our lives. There was never one around where we lived, and this one has just opened today. There are a lot of people, but not as many as I thought there would be.

Leon picks Xander up and lets him sit on his shoulders, making the little boy feel tall.

"Where do you want to go first, squirt?" he asks his brother.

"I want to go on …" Xander looks around and then points. "That one!"

"Are you sure?" Leon says. "Isn't that too scary for you?"

"No!" Xander protests. "My teacher says that I'm really brave!"

"I bet you are," Leon says and then tries to look over his shoulder at us. "Well, you heard the kid. Let's move out!"

"Leon, we're not in the army," I say as I walk next to him.

He puts his finger to his lips and shushes me. "It's for him," he whispers, pointing at Xander.

I smile and play along. "Yes, Sergeant Leon."

Xander giggles and looks down at Leon. "You're a *Sergeant?*"

"Of course!" Leon says glancing up. "And you're the Captain."

"I *am?*" he asks, getting more excited by the minute.

"That's why we're following your orders," I say. "*Captain* Xander."

Rose comes and stands next to me, and Graham goes next to Leon.

"We're going to face a tough adversary right now," Rose says.

"What's an *adversary?*" Xander asks.

"It means enemy," Rose explains. "Do you want to know their name?"

The Captain nods happily.

"It's a very dangerous ride, which they call," she pauses for dramatic effect. "The Pirate Ship."

Xander gasps happily, and Graham joins in the game.

"You have to go through a series of mazes to get to the Pirate guarding the treasure," he explains. "Captain, are you ready?"

Xander nods eagerly.

"Then let's go!" Leon says and begins to run, and we chase after him with Xander laughing and bouncing on his shoulders, with his hands resting on top of his head. I try to keep up the pace without making it obvious that I'm struggling. We arrive at the rollercoaster and Leondre takes Xander down, and we get in line. He and Graham are both trying to entertain Xander until it's our turn.

Rose is next to me, and she leans against the railing while I jump on top of it and sit there, my hands gripping the metal.

"So …" she says. "How're you and Leon?"

"What do you mean by that?" I ask.

"Anything going on between you two?" she asks.

I roll my eyes. "What makes you say that?"

"Graham told me that yesterday when he went to his house, you were there," she says. "And you *never* go there."

"So?"

"And he said that you said that you guys were walking in the park together and *then* decided to go to his house."

"Again, so?"

"Are you guys going out yet?"

"No!" I exclaim. "And what do you mean '*yet*'? It hasn't happened, and it's never going to."

"That's what you say," she says. "But that guy is so in love with you, he's oblivious to any other girl that comes his way. I bet that if Shakira or someone else that teenage boys find pretty walked down this street and wanted to hang out with him, he would stay with us because *you're* here."

"No, if he stayed, he would stay because we're *friends*," I correct her. "Just friends. And I doubt he would stay."

"Then why don't you ask him?" she says.

"Because he'll probably say that he'll stay because that's what he thinks he'll do," I tell her. "But the truth is, if some celebrity walked down this street and wanted to be with him, he would leave me for them faster than ever."

"Don't be so insecure," Rose says quickly.

"If I were *very* insecure, I would say that you don't love me, and I know you do, so don't judge my self-confidence."

It's finally our turn on the ride, and we pile into one of the carts that have six seats, which is just enough. Shockingly, Xander wanted to sit with Graham in the back, so Rose makes me sit with Leon in the front, and she sits alone in the middle. We strap in, one of the staff members pulls a lever, and we're on our way. We go inside a tunnel and are enveloped in darkness so I can just make out Leon's face, but can't see anything besides that.

"You scared yet?" he whispers to me.

"I'm not scared of anything," I say.

"Sure," he says sarcastically.

"Hey!"

"Oh, don't try to be tough," he tells me, and I can tell that he's searching for me in the dark. "Everyone's scared of something."

"Not me," I say, and straighten up a bit. "I'm invincible."

"Aren't you afraid of dying?" he asks.

"Nope."

"Rephrase: aren't you afraid of *how* you die?"

"Again, no."

"Of never finding happiness?"

I scoff. "That sounded so clichéd, you have no idea."

"It's just a question!" he says.

"Are you afraid of that?" I ask.

"No, because I have all the happiness I need," he says. "Right here."

"Right where? In a haunted pirate ship?"

"No!" he says. "You're making this harder than it's supposed to be."

"Not on purpose."

"Again, trying to ignore your sarcasm—"

"Again, impossible,"

"Anyway!" he says, and I laugh. "I mean Xander, and Graham, and Rose, and *you*."

"That's a first," I mumble.

"I mean it," he says. "Have I ever lied to you?"

"I'm pretty sure you have …" I begin.

"Name one time," he cuts me off.

"I just can't think of one right now," I continue.

"Ha!"

"Hey, it could be that you're just saying that because of your bad judgment."

"I do *not* have bad judgment."

"Yes, you do!" I say. "You never see anything bad about anyone."

"How is that bad judgment?" he asks.

"It could be that they lack character, or there's nothing good about them, and you would just be like 'Hey, they have really nice hair,' or something like that."

He laughs. "Like who?"

"If I introduced you to this guy, James, you would probably say that."

Now I know I never said anything about James so far, but that's because I don't *like* mentioning him. He's the worst guy possible. And the truth is, Leon would probably say something like that or compliment his eyes or something. He's just strange that way.

"That depends," he says.

"Meaning?"

"*Does* he have nice hair?"

"Yes, he actually does."

It's only now that I notice that the entire time we've been talking, there have been creepy pirate ghosts popping out, and I hear screams followed by Xander's high-pitched laughter. This just proves how much this guy can distract me. How when I talk to him, I notice nothing else, and it's crazy, it's completely insane, and Rose is right, I *am* mad, and I have proof. Because I'm starting to believe that she could be right about something else too.

Just not yet.

CHAPTER SEVEN

I have gone three whole months barely eating, and I feel a strange sense of accomplishment and an even stranger sense of guilt. I am not used to feeling proud about something, and though I am used to feeling guilty about something, I am not used to feeling guilty about this. I've learned to control my stomach so it doesn't growl randomly when I'm hungry because now my brain just tells it to shut up and it does.

And now I'm beginning to think, 'Hey if I went three months like this, why not six?'

I step on the scale and I weigh 103.5 pounds, and when I measure my wrist, I can loop my hand around it with my thumb and middle finger touching without even trying to. I decide to test it. I can do that without touching the skin on my arm all the way up to my elbow.

This isn't healthy.

I hear Leon's voice in my head, and I want to ignore it, so I hurry up and get dressed to go over to Rose's.

It's December by now, and little flakes have begun to fall from the sky, and even though there hasn't been a full-out blizzard by now, there's going to be one soon. I can tell.

Another summer has come and gone, and so has fall, so it's my junior year. By now I've known Leon and Graham for a little over a year, yet I don't completely trust Leon yet, and I don't know why.

"It's because of the butterflies you get when you see him," Rose had told me. "Once you learn to trust that the butterflies are right, you'll trust him."

"I do *not* get butterflies," I said.

"Sure, you don't," she said. "It's probably a whole stampede."

Of course I had told her to shut up, and, of course, she mentioned it again, but I still don't know whether I should trust the butterflies or not, because what if they're wrong, unlike she says?

My mother met him and liked him a lot, and since she's my mom when he left, she said, "You know, I wouldn't mind him as a son-in-law."

"Mom!" I groaned, and she laughed, so I guess that was her way to tell me to trust the butterflies too, but I still can't. I can't even tell myself that the butterflies are even there at all.

By now, Leon has met that guy James, and he agreed that the guy does have good hair, but he also agrees that he's a douchebag who can't keep his mouth shut. After they had talked, Leon came to me and pointed over to him, and said, "That's the guy? The one who messed you up so badly you can't trust anyone anymore?"

I nodded.

"Nice guy," he muttered sarcastically.

I smiled. "He really knows how to boost your self-esteem, doesn't he?"

"For once, I appreciate your sarcasm."

"My sarcasm should always be appreciated," I said.

"But either way, that's him?" he asked.

"Yep."

He glanced back, and then mumbled under his breath, "Not worth it." As if he would actually do anything.

I walk up the steps to Rose's house and don't even knock on the door. I just open it and go inside, knowing that they're all waiting for me by now.

Leon, Graham, Rose and I planned to meet here today so we could celebrate the week before Christmas together. Rose and I do this every year, and we hesitantly decided to let Leon and Graham join in on the tradition.

"Guys?" I call.

"In here," I hear Rose's voice calling me from the living room, and I go through the kitchen and turn a corner to get there. Leon and Graham are sitting on one couch, and Rose is laying down on another one by herself, saving my spot.

"Hey, Marissa," Leon says, and Graham waves.

"Hey, guys," I say, and sit down next to Rose, and all she does is raise her feet to make room, but once I'm seated, she puts them back down on my lap.

"How long have you guys been waiting for me?" I ask, taking my hat and sweater off.

"I got here, like, just before you did," Leon says. "Literally, I sat down, and then I heard the door open."

"I got here on time, which was fifteen minutes ago or something, so I've been here for a while," Graham says.

"Because fifteen minutes is so long," Rose mutters.

"For me, it is," he says.

"That's because you lack self-control and patience," I say.

"No, I don't!"

"You, do. Don't you agree, Leon?"

Graham looks at Leon, waiting for an answer. "Hate to break it to you, man," Leon says. "But it's kind of true."

"Leon, you really do have bad judgment," Graham says.

"No, I don't!"

"Okay, guys, both things are true," Rose cuts them off. "Graham needs patience and self-control, and Leon has bad judgment."

"We do *not!*" They yell at the exact same time.

"It's okay," I say, pretending to get serious. "Denial is a part of the process to get better."

"Oh, my gosh," Leon says.

"Sending you to therapy will make you get better faster." Rose goes along with it.

"Here we go again," Graham says, throwing his hands up, exasperated, and I notice how often he does that because of me.

"We should start make an infomercial to support them," I say. "We need the money for their treatment."

"Marissa."

Rose cuts Leon off. "We really should. But then we need to save up the money for the psychiatric hospital."

"Guys, no."

"We have been quite worried about you two for quite some while." Rose crosses her arms and looks at them. "It's time we take action."

"Rose," Graham says.

"Graham, tell us exactly how angry and without patience you are."

"Oh, I'm angry and losing my patience all right."

At that point, Rose and I just start laughing so hard, and we can't stop. Graham and Leon are just sitting there staring at us losing our minds and unable to breathe, like, wow, you guys are great friends, just looking at us having spasms. I mean, this could be a legit seizure, and you just sit there like, 'Okay, cool, that's nice.'

"Guys, can you just … calm down?" Leon says.

"Okay, okay, I'm …" I stop mid-sentence and the laughter strikes again.

"Ma-ri-ssa!" Leon says, pronouncing each syllable.

"Le-on-dre!" I stop laughing and mock him.

"Okay, I'm fine," Rose says, finally gaining control of herself.

"You good?" Graham asks, and we nod. "Good. Now, what's this tradition that you two do?"

"Oh, well, Christmas Eve is this Sunday coming up and Christmas Day is on Monday, and today is Sunday," Rose explains. "So it's exactly one week until Christmas Eve. Today, we all go to the mall and buy one present for each other. It has to be five dollars or less. And then we give that present to each other tomorrow. Then we go to the mall again to buy another present for each other. We do that every day until the day before Christmas Eve, and on the twenty-third, we buy the presents we've been planning to buy all along for each other. On Christmas Eve, we don't hang out because then we might be tempted to tell each other what we got. We can text and stuff, but no seeing each other. And on Christmas, we give each other the real present. Got it?"

"Got it," Leon says.

"One question," Graham says. "Is it one present for each person? Including on the last day?"

"It's always been Rose and I doing this tradition," I say. "So I don't know."

"It has to be one for each," Rose confirms. "Otherwise, it wouldn't be fair. So we should get three presents each a day. Except for today when there's none, and Christmas Eve when there's none.

"Okay, simple enough," Leon says, standing up and heading over to the coat-rack to grab his jacket. "Let's go?"

"What's the rush?" I ask, standing up also.

"I need *something* to do!" he says, leaning against the back door.

"Okay, fine, just let me get a water real quick," I say, heading to the kitchen.

"Get me one?" Rose asks.

"Sure," I go to get two water bottles, but since I have to open the plastic cover, I take a little while longer.

When I enter the living room, they already have their coats and scarves on, so I just shove my hat onto my head, pick up my sweater, and we rush out the door. It's freezing.

"You need help with that?" Leon asks, amused, as he watches me struggle to put it on while we walk.

"I know how to put a sweater on, Leon," I shoot back.

"Okay, just making sure," he says.

I pull it over myself and put my hands in my pockets. I feel something there, and I'm sure there was nothing there before. I take it out and look at it.

A root beer lollipop.

I hold it up and look to everyone else. "Who put this in my pocket?"

"What makes you think we had anything to do with it?" Leon asks innocently.

"Leondre, don't lie." I turn to Graham and Rose. "Who put this in my pocket?" I call up to them.

They take a quick glance back at me, look forward again and then point over their shoulder at Leon in complete unison.

I stare at him. "Leondre …"

He puts his arms up in mock surrender. "Fine, it was me."

"And why?" I ask.

"Why what?"

"Why did you put this in my pocket?"

He shrugs. "I just felt like giving you something. And since I'm broke, and the little money I have I need to save for the presents, that was all I could get."

I laugh. "You're so …"

"Weird?" he suggests. "So I've been told. Every day, actually."

"Do I really tell you that every day?"

"Maybe."

"*Maybe?*" I repeat.

"But then again, maybe not."

We arrive at the bus stop right when it pulls up to the curb and climb in when they open the door. There are no spare seats, so we have to stand and hold onto the poles.

"When I get a car, we won't have to do this anymore," Leon whispers to me.

I turn around to face him. "You're getting a car?" I ask.

"Yes, I am," he confirms.

"When?"

"My dad said I could get one for the New Year or my seventeenth birthday," he says. "And once I do, we can go wherever we want to go."

"But do you already have a license?" I ask.

"I've had my permit for a while," he explains. "But I'm taking the final test for my license the day after Christmas."

"December twenty-six?"

He pretends to look confused. "Isn't that what I just said?"

"Is it?" I say. "I thought that you said 'the day after Christmas.'"

"Same difference."

"Same *thing*," I correct.

"You just have to be right, don't you?"

"Yes, I do," I say, and then ask, "Where do you want to go with your car?"

He shrugs. "I've never been out of this state. Not on a school field trip, or anything. Just always been stuck here in boring Pennsylvania."

"So you want to get out of the state?"

"Not only that," he says. "Have you ever been out of the state?"

I scoff. "Man, I've never been out of this town."

"Then you have it worse than me," he says. "Maybe that's why you're afraid."

"Afraid of what?" I ask suspiciously.

"Of a lot of stuff," he says. "You're afraid of never getting the chance to get out of here. You're afraid that people you love will leave you."

When he said that, it just hit me like a ton of bricks, and I'm just thinking, *He has no idea.* But he wasn't finished.

"And you're afraid that you'll never be able to really *live*," he finishes.

"Live?" I say. "I'm alive, aren't I?"

"No, I mean like, do something crazy," he explains. "Something that you can look back on and be proud of."

"Up until now, I got nothing," I say.

"No achievements?" he says. "There has to be *some*thing."

"I'm proud of my childhood," I say. "And I read the entire Chronicles of Narnia in two days. Does that count?"

"That's it?" he asks.

"So far, yeah."

"Then we have to fix that," he says. "But are you *sure* that's it?"

"Well, there was also the time where one of my pictures got published in a magazine," I say. "Is that an achievement?"

"You're a photographer?" he asks, surprised.

"Not really," I say. "Like, I take pictures, and some of them turn out really nice, but I'm not a professional or anything."

"Do you … have any pictures of me?"

"Why do you ask?"

"You've been in my room," he points out. "And you've seen the Polaroid pictures of us on the walls."

"Yes, I actually *do* have some pictures of you. Most of them are group pictures, but there's one that I took last month when you were messing around with my skateboard."

"I didn't see you with a camera!"

"That's because I was using my phone. I can't afford a real camera, are you crazy?"

"Maybe I am," he says. "But maybe that's a good thing."

"But then again, maybe not."

"Anyway, is there anywhere you want to go?"

"I honestly want to go to New York," I say. "I've heard a lot about it. But how about you? Where do you want to go?"

He pauses, looks down at his feet as if it'll give him an answer, and then tells me, "Just … *away*."

I tilt my head and take the opportunity to look at him, but I mean *really* look at him. I have no idea how I managed to become friends with him. If you think about it, it's practically impossible or just very rare for our type of relationship.

Him: not exactly popular, but known around the school and with a lot of friends. A bunch of the girls in school who don't even know him want him as a boyfriend just because he's cute. And truth be told, if they got to him, they would like him even more. Or hate him, depending on what type of guys they like.

And then me: only one friend before him and Graham came along. Insecure, anorexic, and I'm pretty sure that I look like some weird creature from a parallel universe to some people, when really, the worst that I look like is a potato or something. With my round, yet thin, face and black hair up to my ribcage, there you go, that's enough to look bad.

Yet he accepts that. He accepts *me.* Not only does he accept me, but he actually likes to be around me, likes the way I act, which I just don't understand. One time when I asked him that, he just laughed and said, "Well, I guess I'm very selective."

I don't understand it, but maybe that's the whole point. Maybe I'm not supposed to. It could be that it's all about the element of surprise or something like that. Whatever it is, I don't know if I like it or not. But I think I do. I may be curious, but there are some things that have to remain a mystery. Like this.

Like *him.*

The bus stops, we climb off together and walk up towards the parking lot of the mall.

"Should we just run through the parking lot?" Rose suggests.

"Nah," Graham says.

We all stop in our tracks and take quick glances at one another.

And I don't know why I do, I don't know why I risk it, even though I desperately need the exercise, I start running first.

Immediately, I start hearing shouts from behind me, followed quickly by footsteps.

"Hey!"

"Marissa!"

"That's not fair!"

A few more steps, I tell myself. *A few more steps without blacking out, that's it.*

I reach the entrance, but I can tell that someone is right behind me. A random couple holds open the door for me, and I shout to them, "THANK YOU!" as I run by, and I hear the person behind me yell that too, and I can tell by the voice that it's Graham.

I don't stop until I'm in the lobby, leaning against the wall, taking in as much air as I can. My legs start to hurt, so I sit down and pull my knees up to my chest, wrapping my arms around them. The stars that were in my vision disappear.

Graham comes over and sits down next to me, looking just as tired as I am, but we still have a whole day at the mall to go.

"We … really … need … to work … out ... more," he says between gulps of air.

"I … second that," I reply, and he laughs.

Rose and Leon race in just as we stand up, and they both lean forward and put their hands on their knees.

"Can we take a break too?" Rose asks.

"No, this is the punishment for being too slow," Graham says, and she groans.

"Aw," Leon says.

"Get over it," I say. "Let's go."

We head towards the shops, and then Leon suddenly stops.

"Wait," he says. "Aren't we supposed to split into groups?"

Rose face-palms. "I'm so stupid. Okay, Leon and Graham, you guys go. Come on, Marissa, we have some shopping to do."

"Well, you seem happy about this," Graham says.

"Do you even know her?" I ask sarcastically.

"Good point."

"Where do we meet up?" Leon asks.

"In the food court," I say. "We have two hours. Ready? Go!"

Our groups run in opposite directions. When we're sure we're out of their sight, we freeze at the same time and walk slowly, instead.

"What do guys even like?" Rose asks.

"I have no idea," I admit. "This was never a part of the tradition."

"Ugh!" Rose groans and puts her forehead against the wall. "What do they even think about? This was easier when we were planning it."

"You know what they say," I lean back next to her. "Easier said than done."

"I wonder if they're struggling with this the same way we are."

"I'm pretty sure they know what guys think of since, you know … they *are* guys."

She scoffs. "You know what I mean."

"Well," I stand up straight again. "We only have two hours, so we better get started."

"But where *do* we start?" she asks.

"Like I have a clue. Let's just try—okay, not a clothing store because they probably wouldn't want clothes."

"And we don't know their size."

"So that's out. Um … Graham is nerdy, right?"

"In an adorable way, but yeah."

"Yeah, so—wait, *what?*"

"Nothing."

"Sure," I say slowly, still in shock at what she just said; though I'm happy my ship is sailing, but trying to cover it up. "Why don't we try either GameStop or the bookstore?"

"I got nothing better," she turns around and faces me. "Come on."

We head towards GameStop, and once I enter, I realize that even if we know what stores to go to, we don't know what to get them. Or at least I don't.

Rose, on the other hand, apparently knows exactly what they would like. She heads straight for some video game stuff and Star Wars propaganda, which I'm surprised they still have. Really, how popular is that movie? She disappears down an aisle, and I chase after her.

I find her standing in front of an aisle with a bunch of stuff that I don't recognize.

"Mind helping me?" I ask her.

She barely looks at me. "We can't know what we're getting each other, so I can't help you. Sorry."

"But this is for *them!*"

"Yeah, but I'm still not allowed to know."

I groan, walk away from her and then head to a section with some headphones. I stare at them blankly.

I have no idea what to do.

"Rose, I'm going over to the bookstore!" I call to her over two aisles.

"M'kay!" she yells back.

I get out of the store and then begin walking around to wherever I think the used-books store is. Once I find it and head inside, I immediately think, *I'm not leaving this place in a while, am I?*

Once you're with your books and obsessions, there's no going back. But first things first. I have to find a book for Leon and Graham. Then I gotta head to some department store to find a shirt or something for Rose.

I wander around until I find the aisles with old books because I know that Leon loves those the most (besides dystopian). There's not much here that I know Graham would like, so that'll be more of a challenge. I walk up and down, scanning each bookshelf carefully, examining each book, recognizing ones that I've already read and wondering if they'll like it too.

What about that one? I think. *No, he dies in the end, and it's Christmas, so it needs to be happy. This one? No, they leave each other. I never read this one … oh, wait, that author always crushes me, never mind.*

This is turning out to be harder than I thought.

I take a deep breath and breathe in the smell of books and coffee. I so wish I could live here.

I keep looking and finally decide to buy Graham a beanie somewhere else, since I told him he would look good in one, and he agreed to wear it but never bought one. Soon, I settle on a book that Leon would like, and I realize what an idiot I was since the answer was obvious. He told me that he's wanted to read the sequel to one of his favorite books, so I get that one, hoping that he hasn't gotten it yet.

Once I buy the beanie and book, I have to find something for Rose. I know what she would like, but I don't know what *it is* that she would like if that makes sense.

I check my phone for the time, and I realize that I only have thirty minutes until I have to meet them in the food court. I begin to panic until I spot a beautiful red, plaid scarf that she would love. I quickly go to the cashier to pay and then rush out the door, turn a corner, head up the escalator, and arrive at the food court.

To my surprise and advantage, I'm the first one there. I find a table with four seats and sink down in one, only thinking about how I ran all the way here from that store for nothing. I put my head on the table and rest. Thank goodness it's winter break.

A few minutes later, I hear someone sit down next to me. I turn my head, touching my right cheek to the table, only to see Leon looking down at me.

"Hi," he says.

"Hi," I say.

"You seem tired," he comments.

"Well, I ran up here all the way from *Aeropostale* thinking that I was late, only to find that I was the first one. So, obviously."

He gives a half-smile. "And I'm the second, which I'm proud of."

"Oh? And why is that?"

"Because I'm usually late to everything."

"So am I."

He holds up his hand and says, "For the late people who finally succeeded," and I don't hesitate to high-five it.

"We're complete losers," I mutter.

"Complete losers who got here before Graham and Rose," he agrees. "And I take pride in that."

He stares at me a little longer in silence and then tilts his head. "What do you see from that angle?"

"What do you mean?"

"I mean, is it any different from looking straight? Normally?"

"Is anything really normal?"

Ignoring my question, he copies me, except he puts his left cheek down on the table to face me. I look into his hazel eyes and notice that there are small flecks of different colors in them. There are mostly brown spots, but if you look closely, you can see some blue swimming around in the midst of it. Most of the time, it's barely noticeable, but he's wearing this light blue shirt right now that makes it stand out against the hazel and the brown, but you still wouldn't be able to see it unless you were sitting as close to him as I am right now.

I realize that I have been silent, thinking about his eyes for too long now, but he hasn't said anything. That means that his mind must be wandering around too.

"What are you thinking about?" I ask him.

"About the future," he says simply. "About you."

"What about me?" I ask.

He stares at me more, and I feel as if he's seeing right through me.

"I'm just wondering … it's confusing."

"Confusing people understand confusing things," I say. "Try me."

He hesitates.

"Come on, Graeme," I say.

"The first time that we went to the parking lot, Rose said that you began being—what was it—'antisocial' when you were in the eighth grade."

"You remember that?"

"I tend to have a good memory," he says. "That's one of the many reasons I'm awesome."

I laugh. "You're also pretty conceited."

"No, there's a difference between being conceited and having a good self-esteem," he argues. "Anyway, what made you stop trusting people? And how much do you trust me?"

"Sixty-forty."

"What?"

"I trust you sixty percent out of a hundred. That's ten percent more than the last time."

"You didn't answer my first question."

"I was getting there," I say. "I'll tell you the story when I trust you one hundred percent."

"And what will it take to get you to trust me that much?"

"You haven't done much so far," I say. "And I already trust you that much."

"But it's been over a year!" he says. "That's too long."

"I trust you enough."

"If you trust me enough, then you can tell me."

"Nice try."

A confused look crosses his face, and he says, "Sometimes you seem troubled. Depressed."

"Got anything to help with that?" I ask jokingly.

"'Do not be discouraged; do not be afraid,'" he says.

"What?"

"I'm quoting the Bible. You have to trust that God is in control of your life. Once you do, you will see that everything becomes easier to bear."

I look down thinking. Maybe he is right. Maybe God can help me to overcome my fears and doubts. Maybe there is hope for me, and I can become an optimist like him. Maybe.

I hear footsteps and then chairs scraping against the floor. Leon and I both look up to see Rose and Graham collapse in the two chairs next to us.

"What took you guys so long?" I ask.

"Yeah, we've been waiting for a while," Leon says. "Where have you been?"

"We finished shopping twenty minutes before we had to come here, and I bumped into him," Rose explains, breathless. "So we just walked around and hung out, and lost track of time."

Leon and I look at each other, and he raises one eyebrow. I nod, knowing what he means. We'll talk about setting them up later.

"What do you say we grab something to eat before we leave?" Graham suggests, trying to change the subject.

"Why don't we just stop by the corner store on the way home?" Rose says.

"That's better," Leon agrees, standing up. "Let's go."

We all stand up, grab our bags and leave to get to the bus in time. We're in the parking lot when I decide to be extra lazy, make Leon and Graham carry my bags and jump on Rose's back to make her carry me until we get to the bus stop. I have to look over my shoulder every few steps to make sure they don't go looking through my bags to see what I got them. But once we're waiting for the bus and I discover that there's nowhere to sit, I refuse to get off her. Honestly, the only reason I don't latch onto her when we're on the bus and there are no seats left is because she makes Leon stand between us for protection.

She jokingly sticks her tongue out at me like a five-year-old, and I do it back at her as she takes a spot next to Graham holding onto one of the poles. He and Leon simply roll their eyes, already used to our foolishness and stupidity. They try to act like they're mature or whatever when the reason that we're all friends is the fact that we're all stupid and foolish and immature. None of us is even the least bit sane. And we will never grow up.

Never is an awfully long time.

CHAPTER EIGHT

It's Christmas Eve, and I have spent the entire week hanging out with Rose, Graham and Leon. My mom isn't around again today. There was a really bad accident, and she was called in to help. She apologized and said that she would be back by evening, and, of course, I understand, but this is the first Christmas that there's been something like this, where she can't be here with me. Since I have nowhere else to be, I head to the park. I tried texting Rose, but all she sent was a quick reply that she couldn't talk, and when I passed by her house, I saw a Christmas tree surrounded by ripped wrapping paper.

It's freezing outside, and there's snow on the ground, and the sidewalk is frozen and slippery, so it's the perfect weather to take a walk. Little snowflakes begin to fall from the sky, gathering in my hair and on my eyelashes. I'm wearing leather gloves that Leon bought me earlier in the week, and though they do little to protect me from the cold, I put them on because I hadn't yet and felt like I had to.

I tilt my head up toward the pale sky and stick my tongue out, catching snowflakes in my mouth. Sure, it's a little childish, but I honestly don't care. I do this every time it snows, and I like it. No one can change my mind or stop me from doing something if I enjoy, no matter how old I get. I look forward again and keep walking. Most people take my stubbornness as a turnoff, but they should be glad that I'm stubborn. If I weren't stubborn, I would do things the easy way.

And I don't like the easy way.

"Shouldn't you be at your home?"

I look over to the bench and smile. And I thought I would be the only one out here today.

"You know ..." Marcus says. "With your family?"

"Shouldn't you be?" I walk over and sit next to him.

"Nah," he says. "My family is all the way in California."

"They *left*?" I ask.

"They wanted me to go with them," he says. "But I told them no. Because I like it here, and there're people that I love, and I have a good life."

"Working at a drugstore?"

"In case you haven't noticed," he retorts. "I only work three times a week now. Due to my college classes."

"I haven't noticed."

"Because you're too busy staring at Leon."

"What?"

"What?"

I elbow him, and he laughs.

"So you're living alone now?" I ask.

"No, I'm attending a boarding school. So I have one roommate."

"Poor guy."

"What's that supposed to mean?"

"Exactly what I said."

"Oh, shut up!" he says.

"Hey, you're nineteen now, right?" I ask.

"Turning twenty in a few months, yes," he confirms.

"Okay, you know how old I am, don't you?"

"Yes, you turned sixteen a few months ago."

"So, therefore, you're about three or four years older than me?"

"What's your point?"

"And you still hang out with me?"

He pauses, thinking. "Again, what's your point?"

"Don't you have anything better to do?"

He laughs again. "Marissa, once you're in college, you'll understand that there's never anything better for you to do."

"But don't you have some other friends that are—oh, I don't know—your age?"

"I do," he says. "But there are times where I actually like to hang out with people like you."

"People like me?" I repeat. "What's that supposed to mean?"

"It means that sophomores or teenagers, just people your age, have all the time in the world," he says. "Yeah, you're broke. Sure, there can be some backstabbers, but those are the years where you have enough freedom, but not too much. You don't have to worry about a real job or getting married or whatever. You just ... I dunno, get to *live,* I guess."

"I thought that childhood was when you had the most freedom," I say.

"That's what the world makes you think," he points out. "But think about it. Did you *ever,* in your entire childhood, think that the world was selfish and cruel? Or did you try to find rainbows everywhere and see the good in everything?"

"Yeah, I get it, the world sucks. What does that have to do with anything?"

"Right when you hit twelve or thirteen years old, reality slaps you in the face. But that's when the fun begins."

"Marcus, you're confusing me."

"Think of it this way," he says. "In the teenage years, you get reality, which isn't so great. But you also get some freedom along with it. In other words, would you rather have freedom and reality, knowing who are your real friends, or would you rather have a *sense* of freedom, chasing after something that's not real?"

I exhale and bite my lip. "I see what you mean."

"Good, because I didn't feel like explaining that part anymore." He leans back against the bench. "Anyway, reality hits you when you're through ages thirteen or fourteen, but you don't get the freedom, so the years from eleven to thirteen pretty much suck. But then when you're thirteen or so, you begin getting some of that freedom, depending on what kind of parents you have. So then you have five years of that freedom, from when you're thirteen to when you're eighteen."

"And you're nineteen," I say.

"I've used up my last year," he sighs. "That's why I like hanging out with you, or Leon, or Graham, or Rose. I feel like I still have one year left."

"How about college?" I ask. "Don't you have some freedom there?"

"You do, actually, but it's not the same. We sort of have the same thing you do, but there's one difference."

"What's that?"

"We have to deal with the future that is coming faster and faster towards us, and we don't know how to handle it. So we can't enjoy the freedom as much as we'd like. Too much pressure, like I said before."

"What should I do?"

"What?"

"What should I do?" I repeat, more urgency in my voice. "I only have about two years left of the kind of freedom you're telling me about. I don't want to waste it."

"Then don't!" he says. "Live your life, date Leon already, go freaking skydiving or something! But you're growing up, whether you like it or not, you need to accept it. Once you've accepted it, you'll know how to deal with it."

I look down at the cold bench then up at the sky again. He must see my doubt.

"What's wrong?" he asks.

"I don't feel like the freedom is there," I say. "I feel … *trapped.*"

"Once you're out of high school, you'll see it. And you'll regret all the chances you didn't take."

"So?"

"So go for it, whatever 'it' is!" he says and checks his watch. "I got to go. By the way, go to church with Leon already. He's desperate. See you around."

I nod as he stands up. "See you."

He waves and begins to walk away.

I turn my attention to the sky again, maybe Marcus is right, maybe I should go to church with Leon. Maybe I need God more than I think. Then I hear his voice again.

"By the way," he calls to me, and I look at him. "Hurry up and kiss Leon already! Rose and I are tired of waiting!"

"Shut up!" I yell back.

He puts his hands up in surrender. "Just saying!" And then he waves again and jogs towards his car that he parked a few blocks away.

I sigh. Marcus can actually be smart when he wants to be. I replay our conversation in our head.

Wait a second, I think. *When you're that age, you have to think about getting* married*? Wait,* Marcus *thinks about getting married?*

"Of all people," I think out loud.

I replay the rest.

He could've ended the conversation with something deep and thoughtful, but he chose to say that, of all things.

I play the rest of the sentence.

I need to have a talk with Rose.

When I get home, it's around five, and it's already dark out, but the reason I came back is because the snow outside is beginning to turn into a full-out blizzard. I shake off my gloves and scarf and kick off my boots. I'm in the middle of taking off my jacket when I hear light footsteps coming in my direction from the den. I rake off my thick, wooly, red sweater and stay in my loose black shirt. I'm pulling the sleeves down over my wrists when my mother walks in.

"Mom?" I say.

"Surprise!" she says.

"What are you doing home?" I ask, and then try to correct myself. "I mean, not that I'm not happy you're here. It's just that, I thought that you were working today."

She puts her hands on her hips. "Did you really think that I would miss Christmas?"

"Christmas *Eve*."

She waves my comment away. "Same thing."

"So, what are we going to do?"

"Well, every Christmas we usually watch those Christmas movies like *Elf*..."

"What's wrong with that?"

"I know you want to watch something else."

She heads back into the den, and I follow. I look over at the television and notice that it's open on Netflix.

"Pixar movies and reality TV show marathon," she says. "How's that?"

I hug her awkwardly. "You know me too well."

She laughs. "I'm your mother. Of course, I do."

"Okay, I'm just going to go upstairs to change first."

"I'll be here."

I run up the stairs smiling, happy that she could be home with me instead of at work. I open my drawer and pull out my favorite winter pajama pants, which is just a simple red and white striped one. I'm about to rush back downstairs when I hear a buzz from my phone. I reach for it on my bed.

Is silence and noise the same thing? Or does silence scream louder?

It's Leon. And this isn't the first message from him. I scroll back to the first message he sent today.

Are you busy?

Marissa.

Marissa.

So I guess you are busy.

Or you left the house without your phone. That would be a first.

It's also a first where you're silent. Since you usually talk a lot.

I roll my eyes.

Are you talking to someone? 'Cause that would be ironic.

You know, since you're being pretty silent to me right now.

Am I annoying you? Because, I need to annoy you at least once a day. But since I've sent you nine messages so far, then this could end up being a new record.

Ten, now.

"However, they did not listen but stiffened their neck like their fathers."

Quoting the Bible again.

Are silence and noise the same thing? Or does silence scream louder?

My phone buzzes and a new text appears.

Disregard that last text; I was having one of my moments.

I put my hand over my mouth and barely stifle a laugh.

Marissa, I know you're there. My phone has begun saying 'Seen' after every text I send.

That doesn't mean I'm going to stop, BTW.

I decide not to reply, just to see where this will go.

"Marissa?" My mom calls up to me from the bottom of the staircase. "Are you all right?"

"Yeah," I yell back. "Yes, I'm fine. I'm coming."

I stick my phone in my pocket and race downstairs, wondering how long he'll be texting me like this.

I join my mom on the couch, and she looks me up and down for a little too long, and I sense that something's wrong.

"What is it?" I ask.

"If you just had to change your pants, then why did you take so long?" she asks.

"Oh, um …" I bite my lip, contemplating what to tell her and then finally settle on the truth. "Leon texted me."

"You didn't reply, did you?"

I tilt my head at her. "How'd you know?"

She points to my pocket. "I could hear the phone buzzing from down here, and when it didn't stop, I figured that you hadn't replied."

I throw my hands up. "Okay, so I didn't."

"Why didn't you?"

I reach into my pocket and pull out my phone to show her the last texts that he sent me, and she chuckles.

"You want to see where this will go, don't you?"

"Again, how'd you know?" I repeat.

"You shouldn't keep him waiting for long," she says, ignoring my question. "He's going to assume that you are upset at him."

"No, he won't," I say, just as my phone buzzes again. I unlock it, and the messages pops open, and I read it as she does the same over my shoulder.

What did I do this time?

My mother laughs, and I groan and roll my eyes.

"I told you," she says as she nudges me playfully with her shoulder.

"Okay, I get it. But I'm still not going to reply now," I tell her, tucking my phone away back in my pocket. "Right now, we're going to watch episodes, which is what we planned to do."

"You get to pick first."

I grab the remote and type in *River Monsters.* When I'm pressing play, my mom says, "You know, most girls would pick *What Not to Wear* or something with clothes."

"Mom, you *raised* me," I say. "When have I *ever,* in my entire life, been like 'most girls'?"

"I don't want you to be like 'most girls' if that's what you call them. I want you to be *yourself.* Different. Honest."

"*Very* honest."

"Yes, very honest."

She's silent for a few seconds, watching the show, watching what's the next monster this crazy fisherman will catch.

"Why do you like this show so much?" she asks. "Don't the sharks and things scare you a bit?"

"Why, do they scare you?"

"A little bit."

I sigh. "It reminds me of someone. Someone who *really* liked fishing."

"And who would that be?"

She knows the answer. She knows what I'm about to say, I know she does, but she asked me either way. I've been in that position I know why she asked. It's so obvious, yet some people are blind to see something like this. She knows what I'm about to say; yet she knows that I'm hesitant to answer because it's hard to say, hard to just call it out, hard to talk about someone we don't want to talk about, but we do anyway.

"Dad," I say slowly. "It reminds me of Dad."

She looks down, then up at the television and keeps her eyes there. "Me too," she says.

And I know what she means. She doesn't mean that it reminds her of Dad too. Even though I would never say it out loud, even though I'm still too afraid to even tell people about it, and I don't tell people; Rose only knows because I needed someone to comfort me at the time, but when I said that the show reminds me of him and that's why I watch it, my mother knows what I meant; she knows I meant that I miss him and that I love him.

And so does she.

One time she told me that when you say your vows, you say, "Until death do us part," that's a *promise.* A promise that must be kept, that some people keep until even *after* death. She's one of those people. And even though it's hard to believe that I will ever say those words because I don't believe in that whole "true love" thing. I think that it existed once, and that's how my mother and father fell in love and got married, but as time goes on, people stop thinking about who they're going to marry and start thinking about who's the best-looking, or who would boost their ego. That is what has become of our generation. We have been destroyed, in more ways than one, but we still do not get help.

I still do not get help because I do not like to be pitied, I do not like to feel helpless because I'm not, I'm not, I'm not.

I just wish my father was here so I could cry into his shoulder, and he would tell me to be strong and talk to anyone who would even *try* to mess with me.

But he's not here.

And this is the fourth Christmas that I've wished he were.

CHAPTER NINE

I weigh 96.7 pounds.

It's a weird thing to do first thing on Christmas morning, but when I woke up, I ran to the bathroom, stumbling a bit, feeling weak, and stepped on the scale. These are my thoughts now. I weigh as much as I did when I was nine before I was anorexic. I feel clean. I feel like food is now an enemy I cannot let overtake me, and I need to destroy it by throwing it away. I can't consume it or else it would be consuming me. And I'm happy this way. I'm happy to see a small waist and a thigh gap. I'm happy to see a thin face and a tiny wrist. I feel proud when I see my collarbones and hipbones.

I'm so happy that there's *less* of *me.*

My mother has begun to take notice of my weight but never makes me step on the scale in front of her. She told me that I'm very skinny for my age and asked if I've been eating, and I felt as if I could not back down, that I would not flush away two years of eating little-to-nothing down the drain, so I said that I eat the way that I'm supposed to, so I am not lying, but I am not telling the truth. So she just shook her head and said, "Maybe I'm beginning to lose it. I should work less."

Since then, I've started to be more careful. I already wear big T-shirts that do not expose my ribcage and pants that are tight around my waist so they won't fall, but are big around my thighs so it won't show how skinny they are. But instead of just throwing away my food, I started using some tricks I learned.

Instead of putting the food in your kitchen garbage, put it in the dumpster. Run a fork along your lips to make it look like you ate. Wear makeup so you won't look as pale. Try to withstand the cold surrounding you by wearing things that match the weather. But last night, I was home alone and slept in leggings and a tight long-sleeve shirt, and when I look in the mirror, I see the big gap between my thighs; I see how thin my hands are, yet how big they look compared to my arms, no matter how thin they are too.

I examine my face more closely—my long, dark hair, my narrow yet round nose, some very faint freckles, and my plain brown eyes. I am ordinary. The only thing different about me is how thin I am. But I will not stop.

If I have lost this much—if I have gotten to 96 pounds, then why not get to 90?

I step away from the mirror and rush to get dressed. Mr. Graeme bought Leondre a car as a Christmas present to surprise him, and even though it seems old and used, Leondre loves it. He's coming to pick me up to drive me to Graham's house, and even though I resisted at first since it's only a few miles away, I eventually found out that he just wanted to use his new car. So, I said yes to make him happy. When I asked him about Rose, he told me that she said she'd rather take the bus, and though he believes her, I know it's just another one of her attempts to get us to go out.

I take out some sweatpants and a big, long-sleeve, knitted, red shirt that falls off my shoulder sometimes, and just put it on over a tank-top. I shove on a pair of black boots and my leather gloves, then grab my beanie and jacket and the presents `I bought my friends, and then head outside to wait for Leon to arrive.

I pull on my jacket over my shirt and put my beanie on my head just as Leon pulls up. Since he just got his car yesterday, he only told me that it was a bit screwed up, but I can see why he likes it so much. It's a big grey pick-up truck that, honestly, needs some repairing, but it's lovely in my eyes and perfect in his.

He jumps out of the truck, walks over to the passenger's side the same time I do and opens the door for me.

"Milady," he says, bowing slightly.

"Shut up," I say, smiling.

I step inside and sit down as he closes the door. Once he gets into his seat and turns the car back on, he says, "Now, I shall introduce you to my music taste."

"Haven't you already, though?"

"Yes, but I'm going to introduce you to the kind of music that will match both of our styles."

He turns on the radio and switches to a station that's playing some old rock song, and I have to admit I like the beat, even though their voices are a bit weird.

"What song is this?" I ask.

"*Gimme Shelter*," he says. "Even better, this isn't a cover or anything. It's the original. You like it?"

"It's pretty cool. What station is this?"

"No, actually, I just made my own CD of a bunch of songs that I thought we'd both like." He chuckles, looking down and shaking his head a bit. "Stupid, right?"

"Not stupid," I say. "Sweet."

He looks up. "You're not lying to me, are you?"

"No, I'm not."

He holds up his hand. "Pinky promise?"

We've been doing the pinky promise thing for a while now. Rose and Graham have begun to say that we take it so seriously, and Leon and I just feed that idea by joking and saying that a pinky promise is betting off your life. I only pinky promise with him; only him, and no one else.

I loop my pinky with his. "Pinky promise."

He smiles, and then looks forward and begins driving to Graham's house. I hear him humming along to the song playing a few seconds later and glance at him.

"Do you have this song memorized?" I say.

"Just a little bit."

"Do you feel like singing?"

"Yes, and I was just about to start, but let me warn you, I am totally tone-deaf."

He starts singing at the top of his lungs, completely off-tune, and I'm laughing so much my sides hurt.

I jokingly cover my ears and giggle while shouting, "No! Make it stop!" and his response to that is by turning up the volume and singing even louder.

When the song ends and the next one plays, I recognize it immediately.

"Oh my gosh, I love this song!" I say, putting it even louder.

"*You've Got to Hide Your Love Away*?" he says. "You like this song?"

I nod and begin singing. He joins in, and we roll the windows down, annoying the cars that pass us by playing whatever music they're listening to, and we sing even louder when people look at us funny.

How could she say to me

Love will find a way

Gather round all you clowns

Let me hear you say

I look at him, at the way he's smiling and yelling and singing and how he knows every word the same way I do, and his eyes are so bright, and once again he's wearing the blue shirt that I love that brings out the blue in his eyes. He's so strange. Odd. Different, however you want to put it. But I am too. We're both mad.

And that's when I realize that I fell in love with him a long time ago.

When we arrive at Graham's house, they're both already there waiting for us.

I smile as I walk into the living room, kick off my shoes and sit down next to Rose on the couch. Leon goes and sits across from us next to Graham, putting his presents down on the floor. I notice that Graham and Rose have theirs piled up next to them too.

"So, what do we do on this last day?" asks Graham.

"We eat, watch movies, and open presents," explains Rose.

"That's it?"

"That's it."

"Okay," Leon rubs his hands together. "Then what's there to eat?"

Rose slaps her forehead. "I'm an idiot!"

"You know it's not the first time you've said that," I mutter, but she barely hears me as she stands up and fumbles to put her jacket on.

"Rose, what did you do *this* time?"

She glares at Leon. "I forgot to buy the *snacks*! And that's, like, the most important thing!"

The thought of food disgusts me and makes me nervous. I cannot eat, but they will try and make me.

"I'm headed to the drugstore," she says, opening the door. "Graham, you mind giving me a ride?"

He stands up without a moment's hesitation. "Of course," he says, standing up and grabbing the keys to his car and his jacket. He follows her out the door and waves to us. "Be back in a few."

Leon and I are left alone sitting in the living room, and I don't know if this is Rose's second attempt in the day or if she just wants to be with Graham. Could be both. It's most likely both.

I look up only to see Leon's eyes dart away from me, which means he was staring at me. A warm feeling bubbles up inside me and rises to my cheeks, and I pray that they do not turn red with blush. I should not have trusted the butterflies; they are not as trustworthy as I thought.

I can tell that he has now become his bold self again and refuses to look away from me, even when I look up. But now he has been staring more than usual.

"What are you looking at?" I ask.

"You," he says, amused. "That's pretty obvious."

"But *why* are you looking at me?"

He smiles a bit. "Why *not*?"

"Seriously, Leon."

"Seriously, Marissa," He mocks me and then shrugs. "I just like looking at you. Is that weird?"

"Well, yeah, since I'm pretty plain," I scoff. "Like, I would get it if you stared at someone who's, like, a celebrity, or even *Rose* because she looks like a celebrity …"

"What if I like plain?" says Leon. "What if being *perfect* doesn't interest me?"

"Then there's something very wrong with you since most people want perfect instead of plain."

"Perfect is … *so* last year," he says sarcastically.

"Oh, shut up," I straighten up. "That's not normal. You're not normal, Graeme."

He leans closer toward me across the small, black table separating us. "First of all," he says. "You mind calling me by my real name? And second, I take that as a compliment."

I also lean forward towards him. I don't know why I do, but I just do, and I am not aware of my actions or aware of anything, only aware of him, and what he's saying to me, and I am only half aware of my responses.

"I thought you didn't like being called by your real name."

"I want to hear how it sounds like when you say it when you're not mad," he says, resting his chin on his hands. "I'm … curious."

"Wasn't I the curious one?" I ask.

"Yes, and you still are. I just wanted to see what it was like to be curious," says Leon, and then he furrows his brows, thinking. "I was—what was it—I can't remember, gosh!"

He puts his head down in his hands.

I laugh and reach over to ruffle his hair. "You're Leondre the optimist."

He lifts his eyes and peeks up at me. "I haven't been very optimistic lately, have I?"

"What do you mean?" I ask. "You've been acting like … like yourself. What makes you think that?"

"I don't know," he mutters. "I just … don't know anymore."

"Did you know in the first place?"

"What?"

"You said that you don't know *anymore*," I say. "Did you even know in the first place?"

He covers his eyes with his hands. "I thought I did."

"Well, what did you think back then?" I ask. "Maybe you were right."

He looks up again. "How am I supposed to know if I was right?"

"Tell me. I'm usually right."

He scoffs.

"Shut up. Just tell me." I insist.

"I used to think …"

"Think what?"

"You have no idea how hard this is."

"How hard it is to have a conversation? Leon, I have social anxiety. Are you kidding me?"

He groans and lies down on the couch he was sitting on with his hands over his eyes, away from me. "This was so much easier in my head."

Now I'm confused.

"What went easier in your head?" I ask. "Do you, like—plan out conversations in your mind?"

He separates his middle and ring fingers and peeks at me through the hole in between. "Don't you?"

"Well, yeah," I say. "But only if it's a serious conversation."

"And this was *supposed* to end up being serious!"

"And how did that work out?"

He takes his hands away, stands up and walks behind the couch. "You're not helping the process, Marissa!"

"Process?" I repeat. "What freaking process? We were just talking!"

He leans against the sofa. "But I was supposed to casually bring something up and turn it into a deep-talk, and then I got nervous, so you messed it up."

"You're the one who got nervous!" I begin to raise my voice. "How is that *my* fault?"

"You *made* me nervous!" He raises his voice also.

"How can I even do that?" I ask. "I'm just talking!"

"I don't understand—"

"Neither do I!"

"—how you can be so *clueless* and *slow!*"

"I'm sorry for disappointing you with my idiocy," I say. "But you're not making any sense."

"You know what," he walks away from the couch. "Just forget it."

"You can't just drop the subject!" I say. "Now I want to know!"

"Forget it!"

He disappears into the kitchen, and I stand up and go after him.

"And you say that *I'm* the one who makes things difficult."

He stops abruptly and turns to face me. "You actually are," he says quietly. "And I would really appreciate it if you would catch on already."

"Catch on?" I scoff. "Catch on to what? Because honestly, you are talking and exaggerating and arguing about absolutely *nothing*. What is *wrong* with you? I can see what you mean about not being an optimist, but why?"

"I just don't want to talk about this anymore," he says, glancing down at the floor.

I stand there, wondering what got him so upset, wondering what I could've possibly said. He's not one to be quick to get frustrated, especially over nothing. I don't even know how we got to this point. I replay it in my head. There was nothing that I said that could've triggered it. Nothing that he said that could've given me a warning or hinted at whatever it is he wants me to understand. But I don't understand. I can't.

I have been too quiet for too long, and he turns away.

"I didn't think that you would be the type to just explode like this," I say. "With no explanation or reason either. I don't understand it, and I don't understand *you.*"

"Then we're even," he interrupts. "I don't get how one second you're sympathetic and the next you're a hurricane. How does that even ... gah!"

"Could you at least *try* to explain?"

Leon sighs. "I like you. You know that, right?"

"Obviously. I mean you have to like someone to be friends with them."

"Come on, now you *know* you're the one making this difficult," he says. "You know what I mean."

Right on the day I decide to trust the butterflies, this happens. I didn't expect it to be so soon.

On the other hand, it's been almost three years, a voice in my head whispers. I quickly tell it to shut up, and thankfully, it obeys. Partly.

I try to play it off and shrug. "But it's kind of hard to imagine. Let alone believe."

"Why is it so hard?"

"Because I'm, well, me. And you're you."

"What's your point?"

"I guess I don't have one."

"Look," he puts his hands behind his head. "I understand if this is weird for you. It's weird for me too.

I didn't think that I would ever fall in love so easily. I didn't think that I would fall in love with you either."

"Gee, thanks."

"Let me finish."

I stand silently with my arms hanging at my sides.

He sighs. "I like you. I'm confused about it—extremely confused—but I don't know," he shoves his hands in his pockets. "It's kind of a nice feeling, to actually like someone. To actually *love* someone, in *that way*. Love is patient and kind, right? And a whole bunch of other stuff, but I've been *too* patient, and I'm not being very kind right now."

He is telling this to my face. I don't know how, but he has the courage to stand in front of me, tall and awkward, and tell me this. I wish I had that kind of bravery. I still don't know what to tell him. So I ask him something, instead.

"How long?"

Thankfully, he knows what I mean so I don't have to explain it.

He half-smiles, looking at the ground. "Since the day I saw you by the lockers." He glances at me. "I only admitted it to myself the day of the parking lot."

"Oh."

"Yeah, I know," he says and looks up at the ceiling. "*Totally* stupid to tell you *now*, right? First I get frustrated with myself making you think I'm mad at you, and then I tell you this." He heads back to the living room, muttering to himself, "I'm *such* an idiot."

I'm about to go after him when the front door opens. I turn to see Rose and Graham, their faces pink and flushed from the cold, walk in smiling, each with a grocery bag in hand.

I will have to talk to him about all of this later.

Leon is *extremely* good at hiding emotions.

He does not look like he did when we were talking. Before there was confusion and anger, anger not directed at me, but at himself. Now, there is not even the slightest hint of the conversation we had. He is smiling and laughing, and none of it looks forced. His eyes are bright and happy, and he is never distracted or zoned-out. It seems like this is really how he feels.

A thought strikes me. What if this really *is* how he feels? What if everything he said before wasn't true, and he said it as some cruel prank or just to say it? He could be a better actor than I thought. One way or the other, whether it's real or not real, true or a lie, he is a *very* good actor. Convincing, smart, and since he usually always wears a smile on his face, not the least bit suspicious.

I decide to do what I think he's doing and try to distract myself. I think about the presents waiting for us under the trees and get more involved in the game that we're playing, which is just charades. Rose is imitating someone from our school, so I play along and try to guess who it is, but my mind keeps drifting towards Leon. I keep pushing the thoughts away, but it's hard when the reason you want to distract yourself in the first place is right there, eating you up inside.

But soon I forget about it, thinking that it meant nothing. The butterflies don't go away so easily, of course. They're still there, but I just push the thought of them away. Of course, they always invade my mind whenever I see his smile.

Besides that weird conversation, Christmas was good. It was the first one that wasn't just Rose and I giving each other presents when both of our parents had to work. Working on *Christmas*, like they do every year, like they're doing now. I only get to be with my mother on Christmas Eve like yesterday. And since my dad isn't around, it's nice to be with a family that I actually get to spend time with.

For as long as I can.

CHAPTER TEN

I want to sleep for the rest of winter break. I do not want to celebrate New Year's. I want to lie in my bed and forget the world, forget everything. I have been dizzy and nauseous and weak ever since I got back home from Graham's house five days ago. My mom has noticed that I've been paler than usual, and not just because of the cold. She said that my hands are thin, but she hasn't made me step on the scale in front of her. I'm wearing even bigger T-shirts and huge sweatpants or pajamas. Leon, Graham, and Rose haven't mentioned it in a while. Could be because on Christmas I pretended to eat the food they put in front of me. Even though I actually *did* drink the hot chocolate, I now feel disgusting and won't touch anything edible. Just the *smell* of food makes me want to puke.

I roll over in my bed, pull the blanket up to my chin and put my pillow over my head. I am *never* leaving this bed.

Suddenly I hear the front door slam shut. I hear voices downstairs but try to ignore it, assuming it's a coworker of my mother's. And then I hear the thumping of footsteps running up the stairs. I hear them turn the corner and walk down the short hallway.

And then the door to my room swings open.

"Up, up, up!" I hear a voice say.

"Let me sleep," I mumble, still half-asleep. "Five more minutes, Mom."

"Nope. Get up."

She pulls the pillow off of my head, and instead of my mother, I see Leon standing above me, grinning like the a Cheshire Cat, not in the creepy way, but in an extremely adorable way. I am too tired to care.

"Come on, Marissa. Wake up!"

He walks over to the window and pulls open the blinds, and light streams in from outside. The sun isn't out, but the sky is pale, making the room glow enough to blind me.

"Leondre, I want to *sleep*, please."

"No way!" he says, takes the pillow away and throws it on the floor. I quickly pull my blanket higher up to cover my face.

"Marissa!" Leon whines. "Come on!"

"There's nowhere to go, man," I mutter, my voice muffled by the blanket. "You know, there are some days where no adventures await us."

He scoffs. "Impossible. You just choose to believe that and stay in bed."

"For all you know, I could've traveled the world in the past few days."

"No, because you messaged me yesterday and it said 'sent from Philadelphia.'"

"I could've programmed my phone to say that."

"You really couldn't have."

"I really could have."

"I'm willing to bet money that you haven't moved from your bed in three days or more."

"It's going to be far more because I'm not getting up today."

There's a pause, and for a second I think that I may have persuaded him.

"Okay," I hear him say. "Then you won't."

I expect to hear retreating footsteps and my door closing, but instead he moves towards me and scoops me up. I let out a small scream but stay clutching the blanket, so he adjusts it to cover my legs.

"Leon!" I shriek. "Put me down!"

"Will you come willingly if I do?" he asks.

"Um, no."

"Then no."

He walks down the hallway with me still in his arms and heads down the stairs.

"Leon! Stop, put me down!"

"Why?"

"I kind of want to *sleep*!"

"Only because you think there's nothing to do."

"I *know* there's nothing to do."

He pauses mid-step on the staircase. "You complain too much."

"If you're going to insult me, take me back to my bed."

He continues walking down the steps and then passes through the kitchen to get to the front door. I see my mom as we pass by, and she turns to us. Leon stops but doesn't put me down.

"Mom!" I demand or try to, but I'm smiling. "Help!"

She laughs. "I don't see what I can do."

Leon laughs also, and I look from my mother to him and back. "Are you in on this?" I ask her.

"He arrived this morning," she says. "He said you needed to go somewhere, and I agreed. You aren't really sick. I checked your temperature this morning. Fresh air will do you good."

"Yeah, fresh and *cold* air!" I say.

"Do you have her jacket?" she asks turning to Leon.

"Yeah, I'm holding it," he says. "Well, I'm holding it besides her."

"When did you take it?" I ask.

"When you were hiding underneath your covers," he tells me, begins to walk towards the door and opens it. "Bye, Mrs. Anne!"

"Don't forget her shoes!" my mom calls as we head out the door.

"Already got them, thank you!" he calls back and walks to his car that was parked in our driveway.

He opens the door to the passenger's seat, drops me into it and closes the door. Before I can attempt to open it, he locks it.

"Dammit!" I say to myself and hit the dashboard.

He opens the door on his side, hops in, and closes it, laughing.

"What?"

He looks over at me. "I saw that. Pretty frustrated, huh?"

"I feel like I'm being kidnapped," I mutter.

"If you feel like that, then think of it as one of those shows where people think that they're getting kidnapped when in reality they're going to an exciting place or vacation or something."

"There's no show like that."

"I thought there was," he says as he buckles his seatbelt. "They should make one."

"That's true," I agree as I put on my seatbelt also. "Like if they got a whole bunch of teenagers and pretended to kidnap them, put them all on a bus, and then the kidnappers take off their masks, and they're some celebrity and say, 'We're going to Disney World!' or something."

"How about they say, 'We're going to Comic Con!' How's that?" he suggests as he puts the keys in the ignition.

"Oh my gosh, if that were real, I would wish that I could be kidnapped."

"Same." He puts the car in reverse and backs down the driveway.

Once we're on the road, I ask him, "Where are we even going?"

He exhales. "Somewhere you once told me you've always wanted to go." He takes a quick glance at me then looks back at the road. "But never got the chance to."

I furrow my eyebrows in confusion. "You're doing this on purpose."

He smiles innocently. "Doing what?"

"Being all … suspicious, and such."

"Suspicious?" he repeats.

"Yeah," I say. "And sarcastic."

"Suspicious and sarcastic. That's a weird combination."

"Not really,"

"How so?"

"How is it a weird combination in the first place?"

He pauses. "I see your point."

"Exactly."

We're driving down the highway now, and I have no idea where he's taking me. I thought I could've known before, but everywhere that I usually go is within reach, and I never have to take the highway.

"Could you give me a hint?" I ask after a few minutes.

"No need to," he says. "We're already here."

I look around. We're still on the highway, and I don't see any exits besides one that leads to New Jersey. "Where?"

"Here," he pulls into a parking lot of a rest area. I notice a sign that says *Scenic View.*

"But where—" He steps out of the car and closes his door before I can finish my sentence.

He walks to the other side and opens my door. "Did you put your shoes on?"

"Yeah."

"So get out!"

I get out of the car and before he closes the door, he hesitates and asks, "You cold?"

"Leon, I was dragged here in the morning in my pajamas," I say sarcastically. "So yes, I'm quite cold."

"You could use my sweater," he says, already reaching for it.

I freeze. "No," I say quickly. "I brought the blanket too, remember?"

"Oh," he says. "Yeah."

When I look up, I realize where we are. It's the so-called "floating sidewalk" I had told him about so long ago. I can't believe he bothered to remember that conversation that now seems like decades ago.

We begin to head up the ramp, walking next to each other with the blanket wrapped around my shoulders and falling to my ankles.

"It took me a while to figure out what this was called," he admits. "I tried looking up, 'the thing above highways people can walk on,' and that didn't work …"

"Obviously."

He clears his throat overdramatically, and I laugh.

"Anyway!" he continues. "I eventually found out that it was called the highway walkway, or pedestrian walkway."

"Pedestrian is a weird word."

He looks at me funny.

"It is!"

"How so?"

"It sounds like something that's supposed to be offensive," I explain. "Like 'peasant.'"

"'Peasant' is an offensive word?" he asks.

"Well, yeah," I say. "It's as if I'm saying like, 'I'm the queen and I'm above you.'"

He chuckles. "You would be the type to say that."

"I really would," I say. "I used to, actually."

He glances at me surprised. "Really?"

"Nope."

I begin to run up the ramp, stumbling a bit, thanks to the blanket, my clumsiness, and my state of health.

"Hey!" he yells, and then I hear his quick footsteps catching up.

I feel weak, very weak, and dizzy, and the blanket eventually passes my ankles and goes to my feet. I trip over it and fall.

What I didn't notice is that Leon had caught up a while ago and was keeping up the pace, so when I trip, he reaches out just in time to grab my arm and pull me up to face him.

"You okay?" he asks, looking a bit worried, yet amused.

"Yes, I just tripped," I say breathlessly. "Thanks."

"No problem," he says. "But did you have to run?"

"Well, we got to the top faster, didn't we?"

He smiles. "Let's go see how it looks."

Leon turns the corner and goes to the part with metal wires surrounding it. There's a three-foot-tall concrete wall, and then there's the cage, keeping us from leaning or possibly even jumping over the edge. When I look down, I see the cars and trucks racing by, completely oblivious to us. The air is colder, even though we're not so high.

"'You will make known for me the path of life; in Your presence is full of joy; in Your right hand there are pleasures … forever,'" he says after a moment.

"Did you just quote the Bible again?"

"Yes. Anyway, it's really pretty up here."

I close my eyes and take in the sound of everything. If you're able to block out the sound of engines and honking, you can hear the sound of the wind rustling through the little amount of trees there are. It's somehow peaceful.

"It really is," I agree.

"Why did you want to come up here anyway?" he asks.

"It's a pretty stupid reason," I say.

"I live for stupidity. Try me."

I sigh. "Okay, well …" I try to collect my thoughts. "I've never been in a plane before. I only go high off the ground when I'm on a rollercoaster, and I can't be still on a rollercoaster. So I wanted to be high up so that I could be still and above everything else. And maybe if I stand here long enough, I'll feel like I'm floating," I glance at him. "See? Stupid, right?"

He shakes his head. "No. Not stupid. It actually—" he looks around, down at the cars through the fence, and then back at me, "—makes perfect sense."

I smile. "When does anything I say ever make sense?"

"Maybe to everyone else it means nothing, or they don't understand it, but to me," he says, "it's crystal clear."

My heart begins to beat faster and my palms begin to sweat, and at first I think that it's because I'm nervous or because of the way he's looking at me, so I look away. But when I don't calm down, when I begin to find it harder and harder to breathe, I realize that this isn't normal, that it is not because of him but because there is something wrong with me. My heart races even faster, and it seems like there is no air and I am being suffocated. I am gasping for air, but there is nothing; there is nothing.

I am becoming nothing.

"Marissa?" Leon asks, concerned. "Marissa, are you okay?"

I want to tell him no; I want to tell him that I am not okay, that I need help, but no words come out; there is nothing I can say when there is no oxygen. My heart keeps going, faster and faster yet, and I want it to stop, but then I don't because I don't want my blood to stop pumping.

What is happening to me?

Black spots begin to cloud my vision, and I can't … I can't think. My thoughts are only internally screaming at me.

"Marissa?"

I feel my legs go numb, and I fall. Leon catches me and lays me down, still calling my name, wanting me to answer. And I want to answer; I don't want him to worry about me, but it's too late for that when he's been worrying about me since we first met.

"Marissa!"

My eyes feel heavy and begin to close, no matter how hard I try to keep them open, no matter how much he is begging me to stay awake.

I see him fumbling for his phone and dialing in 911. I hear his desperate voice quickly explaining the situation, but I can't stay awake much longer.

He notices me giving up, so he stops talking to the operator long enough to look at me and say, "Marissa, please hold on. They're on their way, so try to relax, okay? Just … stay alive."

I look at him one last time, and then my eyes close, but I still hear the last thing he says.

"Please, Marissa. *Please.*"

And then it seems like the movie has finished and the credits have ended, and there is nothing but a black screen.

When I awake, everything is a blur. I can't make out any faces and am only half-aware of what's going on. The only thing that reminds me what just happened is the mask on my face breathing air into my lungs for me and the fact that I'm laying down but moving, being rolled down the ramp on a stretcher. All the sounds around me are muffled, except for this high-pitched ringing that I can't distinguish.

I feel pain in my chest and in my arms, and I see people dressed in white. Four of them reach down and lift the stretcher into the back of a van. An ambulance.

Where's Leon? I think. That's the first thought to register in my brain.

And then I see him, sitting in a seat in the ambulance, and when he sees them putting me in there, he stands up and comes closer to me. My vision is still blurred, but now there are small moments where it's all clear. And I can barely hear his voice with an eerie echo added to it, but I try to make sense of him.

"Marissa," he says, staring at me, his face full of concern. "Marissa, I'm right here."

One of the people dressed in white, a doctor, I assume, turns to him and says something. He responds but doesn't look away from me. I catch a few words here and there.

"In critical condition," from the doctor, and then it's muffled. "Unhealthy … wasn't surprising … heart attack."

Heart attack.

I am sixteen years old.

And I almost killed myself.

I look into Leon's eyes and see his tear streaked face. I don't want him to worry about me. I wish he had never met me, never had to deal with me, with any of this. I want him to wake up tomorrow morning with no memory of what happened over the last two years, or at least with no memory of me, I don't care. I just don't want him to feel pain. I don't want him to care. He *can't* care; at least he's not supposed to.

Please, I think, hoping he could read my mind. *Please forget about me.*

"You're going to be okay," he says. "You'll be okay."

I am slipping away, and I want to stay awake, I want to talk to him. But I can no longer hold on. The ringing sound begins to fade at the same time my vision does, and that's the moment when I realize the sound was in my ears all along.

I take one last look at Leon's face before I am once again ripped away from reality.

I see that pain that I want erased from him. I want him to be happy, even if it's without me.

And even though I know he's begging me to be okay, I'm also silently begging him to be.

CHAPTER ELEVEN

I was in the eighth grade.

I was thirteen years old.

Rose was my best and only friend.

I had a crush on James Carter.

"Just talk to him!" Rose told me. "He *totally* likes you!"

"I can't!" I said. "He doesn't even know I exist."

"Lies!" she exclaimed. "He's always staring at you."

"That's kind of creepy."

"I mean in the way you look at him during English."

"That's better."

She sighed and glanced over at the table next to us. "Why do all the cute boys have to be such *jerks*?"

"Not *all* of them," I said. "Who knows? Maybe the right guy is sitting at the table you're totally-not-obviously staring at."

She threw a napkin at me. "Shut up."

"But Andy likes you!"

"I'm also a unicorn."

"Unicorns are overrated," I said. "And overused."

"Then I'm a ferret," she smiled.

"Those are also overused."

"Then what do you expect me to say?" she said, throwing her hands up. "That I'm a Portuguese Man of War?"

"Better," I said. "Except you're not Portuguese or a man."

"I'm done," she said and leaned her head against the table while I laughed.

"You guys belong together," I shrugged. "It's *true love!*"

She looked up at me. "You know what else is overrated and overused?"

"What?"

"True love!" she grumbled and put her head back on the table.

"Come on, Rose!" I said. "Lighten up! You actually have a major chance with Andy while with James … I have none."

She straightened up and rested her chin on her left hand. "But you guys talked until ten last night!"

"So?" I said. "He doesn't even look my way anytime else!"

"Because guys are confusing that way," she said and looked at the table they were sitting at again. "He's just playing hard-to-get."

"But that's *my* job!"

"Well, he's stealing it, and you're left unemployed."

I groaned. "This isn't fair, man!"

"I'm a girl, not a man."

"I know that."

"Anyway!" she said. "You're talking to him after school."

"Sure, I can just text him right now," I said, reaching for my phone.

"No," she said. "I mean, *in person.*"

I scoffed. "Yeah, right! Are you insane?" "No, I'm just helping my friend find love."

"I'm *thirteen!*" I exclaimed. "I'm pretty sure that love doesn't exist for my age."

"We're going to find out then, aren't we?" she said raising one eyebrow.

"Okay, I'll talk to him, on one condition."

"Which is?"

"You talk to Andy,"

Her eyes widened. "Are you insane?"

"No," I leaned back against my chair. "But you are."

"Fine, I'll talk to him."

"I was praying you wouldn't agree to that."

"Well, I just did," she said. "So someone's going to have a deep talk with their love today."

"Shut up," I said, threw my plastic fork at her, and she laughed.

"Hey."

I turned around and looked over both shoulders to make sure he wasn't talking to someone else. Everyone was minding their business and walking past us. But still when I turned back to him, I pointed to myself and asked, "Me?"

He nodded and leaned against the locker next to mine. "Who else would I be talking to?"

I smiled, embarrassed. "Sorry. Um, what's up, James?"

"Nothing, right now," he said. "But uh, I was wondering if maybe after school we could go somewhere to grab a bite to eat?"

Is he asking me out? I asked myself.

I looked into his eyes and saw honesty, hope, and nervousness.

Oh my gosh, he's asking me out.

Calm down, Marissa. It's just to go eat.

"Yeah, of course," I said. "Where?"

"There's this new frozen yogurt shop downtown," he told me. "We could go there."

"Okay, sure. Do I meet you there, or …"

"Yes, that works," he smiled at me. "I'll see you later then."

He walked away, and I muttered under my breath, "See you," even though I knew he wouldn't hear.

The bell rang, but I rushed down the hallway towards the bathroom instead of class.

I was flying inside, and I couldn't wipe the smile off my face. I already talked to him that day like Rose told me to, and ever since then we'd talked pretty often, but I still wasn't used to him coming up to me even if it's just to say hi. But that was the first time we'd be hanging out outside of school besides texting, which doesn't really count.

And the fact that *he* asked *me* when I was sure it would be the other way around, made it all even better.

I looked in the mirror and saw my bright eyes, big smile, and breathless face.

I didn't think that anything could ruin my day.

After school, I headed out of the building and walked the two blocks to the city bus stop. James had texted me two minutes before and told me he had just arrived there. That was when I began to have a panic attack and hurry up.

I waited impatiently for the bus to arrive, and when it finally did and I climbed on, I practically threw the money at the driver and sat down in a seat in the back. I already texted my mom, telling her that I was meeting a friend somewhere so I would be home later, and she said that it was okay and to be back before sundown. Of course, I said yes because I didn't plan on staying that long. And I was pretty sure that he didn't either.

I arrived at the shop five minutes later and practically ran inside, walking the last few steps to compose myself and because if he saw me through the window rushing like that, I would die.

Once inside, I scanned the booths to find him and saw him sitting on one of the stools next to a table. His back was turned to the entrance, so he hadn't seen me yet. I smiled to myself and then walked over, my heart beating faster with every step I took closer. I pulled out a chair next to him, and he turned to me as I sat down in it.

"Hey," he said, smiling at me. "I almost thought you ditched me."

"And why would I do that?" I said, trying to be cool when really I was having trouble to calm my breaths and heartbeat.

He shrugged. "Figured that you thought it wasn't worth it."

"Worth what, exactly?"

"Worth even coming, I guess," he said.

"I don't see how it wouldn't be," I replied.

"Let me think," he said, pretending to be deep in thought. "I'm a complete loser, and you're one of the prettiest girls in school."

I scoffed and hoped it didn't show that I was blushing. "Are you kidding me? My only friend is Rose, and no one even pays attention to me unless it's to judge me. You sit at a table *full* of friends and people you can rely on."

"Okay, I see your point on where I sit and who I hang out with," he said. "But in all honesty, I'm an idiot and a jerk."

"You are not."

"Yes, I am."

"Well," I sighed. "I guess I'm going to find out after this, aren't I?"

He laughed. "See, this is something that I like about you."

"What is?"

"You're bluntly honest. And when you're not, you put a small sugarcoat and that's it. But at the same time, you're not mean or rude or anything. It's different."

"Is different … okay?"

He smiled. "It's perfect."

I smiled shyly and looked at the tabletop, hoping he didn't see me blushing, knowing that my face was bright red.

"You want to order?" he asked, pointing to the register.

"Sure," I said, already reaching for my wallet in my purse.

"No, let me. I brought you here, I should pay."

"It's fine, I can do it."

"No," he insisted, already holding twenty bucks in his hand. "Allow me."

James jumped down from the stool and headed to the cashier. I smiled to myself. It was surprising he would want to hang out with me, that he even noticed me in the first place. Most of all, who would've thought that the most popular guy in school could be so down-to-earth and sweet?

He glanced back at me over his shoulder and smiled, his blue eyes lighting up. I smiled back.

I assumed I just got lucky.

"Dad?" I called out when I got home. "Dad, are you here?"

My mom appeared from the kitchen. "Hey, honey. Your father went out somewhere."

I rolled my eyes as I kicked off my sneakers. "Somewhere?" I repeated a bit accusingly.

She sighed. "He was already gone when I got back. He just left a note."

"Saying he went to buy eggs or something when we know where he really went," I snapped. "What's the point of lying? We already know!"

"No, this time he told the truth."

"He said he was going to Tom's?"

Tom was my dad's supposed best friend. And since we didn't let him smoke here, he went over to Tom's, who let him smoke on the patio. He didn't approve of it, but at the same time didn't want to "let his best friend down," which was just plain stupid.

"Yes, he did," my mother said.

"Could I see the note?" I asked.

"I already threw it away. What do you want for dinner?" she asked, changing the subject.

"I already ate, remember?"

She gave me a look. "You went to a frozen yogurt shop."

"They had sandwiches there, and I took one."

"Okay, then," she said, heading back into the kitchen. "Do you have homework?"

"Yeah," I called back. "I'm going upstairs to work on it, okay?"

"Okay."

I ran up the steps and headed into my bedroom. Once I slammed the door shut, I threw my backpack on the ground and pulled out my phone. I had a text from Rose.

Hey, you busy?

I quickly typed in a reply.

Nah, I just got home. Why?

I tossed my phone onto my bed and reached into my drawer for a change of clothes: sweatpants, T-shirt, oversized hoodie. No need to look cute when you're not trying to impress anyone.

Right when I pulled off my shirt and was putting on the other one, my phone buzzed. I finished changing and then reached for it.

Think you can come over? Since we didn't get to hang out before ...

Yeah, my mom won't mind. Be there in two min.

K.

I pulled on my sweater, shoved my phone into my pocket, grabbed my backpack, and ran back down the stairs.

As I put my shoes back on, I shouted, "Hey, Mom? I'm going over to Rose's house!"

"Sure thing," she said. "Did you do your homework?"

"I'm going to do it at her place," I opened the door. "I'll be back later!"

"Okay, love you."

"Love you too, bye."

I stepped outside and closed the door, then started the walk to her house, which was just around the corner.

Once I got there, I didn't even bother knocking, I just walked in.

"Hey, Rose, I'm here," I said, loud enough so anyone in the house would be able to hear.

I heard footsteps racing down the hallway, and Rose appeared a second later, sliding on her socks and almost falling.

"Hello!" she said. "Come on, let's go to my room."

"Did you finish the homework?" I asked as we walked down the hallway she had just come from.

"Yeah, did you?"

"No, I had just gotten home when you texted."

"Oh, yeah!" she said. "I forgot."

"Forgot what?"

"That you were busy with your *boyfriend*."

"He is *not* my boyfriend …"

"Not yet."

"And you didn't forget, you were just looking for the opportunity to bring it up."

"You know me too well."

We entered her bedroom, and I closed the door behind me. I dumped my bag on the floor and once again took my shoes off, which was the second time in the past ten to fifteen minutes.

"Do you have the answers for the math?" I asked, lying down on my stomach on the floor.

"Just copy off mine and tell me everything that happened," she said throwing her homework at me.

"This is why we're friends."

"Because I'm amazing, I know, now tell me!"

"Why does it matter?" I said, looking through my stuff for a pencil and my folder.

"How can you even say that?" she exclaimed, lying on her back and staring at the ceiling. "You went on a *date* with freaking *James Carter,* the most popular guy in school!"

"It wasn't a date," I said. "I'm thirteen. We're just friends!"

"Yeah, extremely good friends who act like a couple. Now, what did you guys talk about?" she asked, beginning the interrogation.

"Just about school and stuff."

"What's the cutest thing he did or said?"

"Well, he said I was one of the prettiest girls in school and that I'm different."

"Is different a good thing?"

"That's what I asked, and he said different is perfect."

Her eyes widened. "You know what that means, don't you?"

"Um, it means that he complimented me?" I guessed.

"He called you perfect."

"He has really bad judgment then."

She rolled her eyes. "Accept the compliment! Please tell me you accepted the compliment."

"Technically, yeah."

"What do you mean by 'technically'?"

"Well, I looked away and blushed."

"Okay, that counts as accepting it."

"It does?"

She threw her arms up, exasperated. "Do you know anything about relationships?"

"No!" I said. "I don't know anything about any of this!"

"Then let me help you," she said, "by giving some advice."

"And what advice would that be?"

She leaned closer towards me. "If you don't screw this up, he actually *could* end up being your boyfriend."

"What if I don't want one?"

She shrugged. "Then it won't be a relationship. It'll just be some kind of screwed up love."

"I'm pretty sure love doesn't exist for my age."

"It exists for everyone, dude."

"There's different kinds of love," I explained. "I'm saying that the kind of love where two people care for each other. That way doesn't exist for me." "Don't be stupid."

"I'm not!" I said. "I just ... ugh! This is hard to explain."

"I'm your best friend," she said. "Even when you sound ridiculous and gibberish, I understand."

I sighed. "Okay, it's just that … if a little kid goes up to you and says that they're in love, what would you do?"

"I would laugh at their adorableness."

"That's it?" I asked, staring her down.

"I would also laugh at the idea that they could possibly know what love is."

"See, that's how it would look like if I went up to an adult and said that I know what it is too," I said. "They don't take us seriously when we say that kind of stuff. They laugh, waving away the idea that we could know what they don't."

"They don't know what it is either?"

I thought about my parents at that moment; thought about how they're still married and how my mother hadn't given up on my dad even after he wouldn't stop smoking. He knew she hates it, but my mom still had hope he would quit some day. But is that really love, when one of them keeps doing the same act of betrayal while the other keeps holding on, praying they'd come around? I couldn't be sure.

"I don't think any human being does," I said.

"Maybe we could discover love again," she said, turning over and laying with her head hanging off the bed, upside down.

"Now if someone older heard this conversation, they would laugh," I pointed out.

She thought it over in her mind. "Why don't they take us seriously?"

"Because they think they know better."

"What if they don't?" she asked, practically demanding an answer as if I had one. "What if, just this once, we know better than they do?"

"They wouldn't believe us if we said so," I replied.

She sighed, stayed silent for a while and then said, "Sometimes I hate being this age. You're too young to know what to do with your life, too old to play games."

I scoffed. "Someone's having a midlife crisis."

"Midlife?" she repeated. "I'm thirteen!"

"My point exactly." I stood up, reached over and shook her by her shoulders. "Stop over exaggerating!"

Rose pushed away my hands and sat up. "I'm not over exaggerating, I'm over*thinking!*"

"Yes, but that leads to over exaggerating, so *stop!*"

"Okay!" she giggled and put her hands up in surrender. "I'll stop. For now."

I rolled my eyes. "But tomorrow?"

"Tomorrow brings a whole new day of overthinking. You should know that more than anyone."

"I know."

Fast forward.

Pause.

Here. Right here.

Play.

James and I had been talking and hanging out after school for three months. Some people said that we were "going out" but I didn't really consider it that. I thought that, being thirteen, it was too young an age to commit to something supposedly official. I believed that for him.

Not for myself.

"What do you want to be when you grow up?" he asked me randomly one day.

"Why do you want to know?" I replied.

He shrugged. "Just to know."

We were taking a walk in the park together, me carrying my skateboard in one hand, him carrying my backpack because he offered and insisted when I refused. I eventually gave in and let him, happy to take the weight off my back. It was a chilly day at the end of January, and there was some snow on the ground. I was riding my skateboard before and showing some tricks until I slipped on the ice and fell. Well, almost fell. He caught me.

"You'll laugh," I said.

"I will not!" he defended himself, pretending to look offended.

"I dunno …"

"What is it?" he asked, very excited at that point. "The next Tony Hawk or something? I wouldn't laugh at that! You take skateboarding very seriously!"

I laughed at his eagerness. "That would actually be a pretty good option, but no."

"Then tell me!" he said. "The suspense is *killing* me!"

"Okay, um … I'm going to be honest with you, I don't know what I want to be."

"You kept me wondering for *nothing?*" he demanded, smiling.

"Let me finish!" I said. "I don't know what I want to be because I haven't thought about it much. You know why?"

"Um, I'd like to!" he exclaimed, throwing his arms up.

"Because I don't want to grow up," I said. "So I'd rather not think about it. But if I had to pick, I would want to be a writer. Of poetry."

"I never thought of you as a writer."

"Well, now hopefully you will."

"I already do."

We walked in silence for a while just breathing in the cold air and enjoying each other's company when I turned to him and said, "How about you?"

"What?"

"What do you want to be?"

He put his hand under his chin and pretended to be thinking really hard. "Hmm …"

"It can't be that hard for you."

After a few more seconds of him lost in his thoughts, he smiled at me and said, "An actor."

"An actor? Isn't that a bit far-fetched?"

"Hey, dream big, you know?" he told me. "It's a possibility. And, you've seen me in the school plays, right?"

"Yes, I have."

"And am I good at acting?"

"You are."

He clapped his hands together. "Then I have a chance."

"Then let's hope you'll be a good one on the big screen," I said.

"Oh," he said. "I will."

We didn't talk for a week after that.

He didn't text me at all, and the one time I worked up the nerve to type in, "Hey," he didn't reply, even though it said *Seen* right under it five minutes later.

He practically avoided me in the hallways, going to his other friends, and he always seemed to be busy every time I contemplated whether I should approach him or not.

"He's probably exactly what he seems like," Rose told me. "*Busy*. If he could hang out with you, he would. Trust me."

But he didn't. My life just seemed to be getting worse and worse. My dad was diagnosed with lung cancer and ended up in the hospital. It had been there growing, and we didn't even know it, he didn't even notice it. My mom had been crying. She tried to hide, but I could hear her crying during the night, and in the morning her eyes were red. She had been working a lot, and when she's off she was in the hospital with dad. So I had to keep living my life as if everything was fine, but it wasn't, it wasn't, it couldn't be, not when my whole world was falling apart.

I went to visit dad in the hospital and instantly regretted it. There were so many tubes attached to his arms and a cannula to help him breathe. Sometimes when he coughed, he would cough up blood. He had these bruises on his body, and he was so pale, so fragile. My dad had broken.

Or maybe he had been that way for a long time, and we never noticed.

He was asleep most of the time I was there, and the doctors told me not to wake him up. I understood. I wouldn't want to wake up either. If he were awake, he would be aware of all the pain around him, slowly reminding him that reality was still there.

I don't like reality.

I sat there, holding his hand, just keeping him company. I wanted him to be okay. I wanted him to be better.

"I'm sorry," I whispered, even though I knew he couldn't hear me, and people would tell me that it wasn't my fault, I felt like it was. I mean, how could it not be? I didn't do enough to make him stop smoking. In fact, I pushed him away for most of my life. I knew that he was addicted to smoking; I knew that most people thought that I was powerless to do anything, but they're wrong. I could've done something. I could've begged him to stop, thrown away the cigarettes, gone for help. I did nothing. I just watched him slowly kill himself, oblivious to what he was doing. Unaware.

I couldn't even look at him anymore with the guilt. I gave his hand one last squeeze, whispered, "I love you," and left, unable to cry, but wanting so badly to get some of the pain out.

A few more weeks went by, and James still didn't talk to me. I eventually couldn't take it anymore. I was done with everything, and I just wanted to talk to him. So when he was at his locker, alone for once, I walked up to him to confront him.

"Hey," I said.

He turned, looking shocked to see me, then made sure no one was around. Then he looked back at me and didn't look away. It began to freak me out. He just stared at me, not saying anything back.

"Um," I cleared my throat, not wanting the moment to get any more awkward. "Why haven't you been talking to me?"

He scowled at me and turned back to his locker. "Isn't it obvious?"

His voice made me nervous. His words were cold and cruel. "What do you mean?" I asked.

"Do I need to spell it out for you?" he said harshly. He glanced at me and put emphasis on the words he spoke next. "I'm done with you."

I stayed silent, and when it was clear that I didn't understand, he rolled his eyes at me.

"I never liked you," he continued. "The only reason I ever talked to you in the first place is because they thought you were a freak."

"They?" I repeated. "My friends," he explained. "They wanted to know if it were true and decided I would be the perfect decoy. I went along with it. My job was to get to know you. I had to be this … fake *gentleman* or something that did every little thing for you to give in.

It worked out better than I thought. And I found out exactly what my friends wanted to know about you."

I stared at him, not knowing what to say, what to think, how to react.

He glared at me, his eyes boring holes into mine. "You really are a freak."

There. His words stabbed me like little needles digging into my skin, and I was done. Done with everything, done with people hurting me, just *done.* I thought he cared for me, and he just stabbed me in the back.

But he decided to make it worse.

"You—you only have one friend, you're failing in school, you don't do anything besides skateboarding," he said. "And you don't know how to accept compliments. Why don't you try saying 'thank you,' if someone says something nice? Even better, why don't you just go to your house and die already?"

I blinked, still frozen in shock.

He yelled, "What is *wrong* with you?"

"What's wrong with *me?*" I shouted back, snapping out of my daze. "Look at who's talking! What kind of sick person leads someone on? Even if it is for so-called friends, there is absolutely no point in it! What could you possibly have gained from this? A boost for your ego? Pride?"

I swallowed and looked down for a second, my voice beginning to break. I could not cry in front of him. I would not give him the pleasure of seeing me break down. My anger began to boil up inside of me, and I looked him in the eye.

"You should take a really good look at what you lost. You lost a friend who wouldn't have betrayed you the way you did me," I continued. "You're nothing but a *coward* and a *liar*."

He glared at me, waiting for me to continue, knowing that I wasn't finished. I couldn't continue much longer, I knew that much. I could feel heat creeping towards my cheeks, and my vision was beginning to blur, but I didn't look away.

"You know, I didn't think that you actually meant it when you said that you wanted to be an actor," I told him. "But it turns out you're going to be a damn good one."

And then I turned on my heel and walked away. But he continued talking.

"Therefore, for my final act," he shouted, "I will reveal the real Marissa Anne,"

I kept walking.

"Who deserves to go and join her father on his deathbed."

I froze.

James Carter had reached a new low. And who knows? Maybe he was right.

And so I ran.

I didn't know where I was going, but I just wanted to get out of there. I walked down the hallway, turned a corner and headed into the first room I could find. I closed the door behind me, locked it and slid down to the floor, pulling my knees up to my chest. I willed myself not to cry, but a few silent tears escaped from my eyes. It was only then that I noticed that the lights were off in the room, and there were no windows.

"Rough day?" I heard a voice say through the obscureness.

I popped my head up and squinted through the darkness to try to see who was talking to me, but my eyes wouldn't adjust and the blur of my tears weren't helping.

The voice chuckled softly.

"What?" I asked the shadows.

"The way you're squinting," he said, obviously used to the darkness. "It makes your cheeks puff up a bit."

"I can't even see you, and you're already making fun of me,"

There was silence, and I could tell he was shaking his head. "No," he said. "It's cute."

"Shut up," I said.

"You don't like teasing, you don't like compliments," he stated. "You're a very picky person."

"You don't know me,"

"So let me introduce myself."

I heard footsteps and a faint light flicked on, bright enough for me to find a curly-haired boy with a cheeky smile and adorable dimples.

"Name's Taylor," he said, coming towards me and extending a hand. I hesitantly took it and stood up to face him.

"And you are?"

I released his hand and cleared my throat. "Marissa."

He grinned and crossed his arms. He leaned a bit towards me. "It's nice to meet you, Marissa."

I will not let him in; I will not let him in …

I didn't respond. I looked down at the ground and tried to swallow the lump still in my throat.

I could feel his eyes studying my probably still red face and his smile disappeared.

"You were crying," he said.

I wiped away some of my tears and glanced up at him. "I'm fine," I replied, knowing that wasn't convincing. "You know what fine means, right?"

I shrugged.

"It means Freaked out, Insane, Nervous and Emotional."

I blinked. "Yeah, so like I said, I'm fine."

"In both ways?"

"Just the second."

"Ah," he sighed as if he understood. He looked into my tired eyes hopefully. "You want to tell me about it?"

"I just met you," I pointed out.

"But I can tell that you're a lot like me," he said, taking a step even closer. "You're afraid to open up because you came running in here after being hurt. Hurt by someone you thought was close to you, who stabbed you in the back. You came into the first room you could find, so they wouldn't see you break down," he raised his eyebrows. "Am I right?"

On point, I thought, but out loud I just simply said, "Or maybe I'm not telling you anything because I just met you.

He half-smiled, amused, probably at my rudeness. "Exactly. If you've never met me before, what makes you think I know any of your friends? Or anyone important to you? I mean, I'm a loser who locks himself up in the darkroom because he has no life."

So that's what this place is ... I looked around but could only see the faint outlines of pictures hung up on strings. They were shiny and appeared to be wet.

"Why *are* you in here?" I asked.

He grinned. "You tell me your life story, I tell you mine."

I smirked. He was smart, somehow knowing how curious I was and that my curiosity always won out, no matter what.

He walked over to a small table with stools surrounding it, and papers scattered all over it with a single Polaroid camera sitting on top. As I stepped closer, I saw that the papers were more pictures. I looked at him, and he patted the stool next to him.

"You're not going to leave me alone here, are you?" he asked raising one eyebrow.

I smiled.

And then I gave in and told him everything.

His name was Taylor Holloway.

He was in my grade, not in a single one of my classes, which would explain why I had never seen him before.

He took photography, and it was his passion. He spent most of his hours in the darkroom, sometimes even stayed after school until nine working in here.

I laughed when he told me that. "You're addicted," I said.

"I'm not even going to deny that," he replied.

When I asked how he knew how I had gotten in there, he said, "Because that's the same way I found this place."

My eyes widened. "Really?"

He nodded. "Last year, I had discovered that my so-called group of friends were telling everyone I was adopted," he looked down at the floor and sighed. "People began calling me 'homeless', 'unwanted', 'freak', 'foster kid', 'charity fund', and a whole bunch of other stuff. It blew over eventually. But that day I couldn't take it, and ran in here. Cried my eyes out."

I didn't take my eyes off him, urging him to go on, silently telling him that I was listening, that I cared.

"Once I stopped crying," he continued. "I decided to explore the place. Flicked on a light switch, and found a bunch of dusty cameras and old pictures," he paused, remembering. "They were beautiful. I fell in love with it. A teacher, who no longer works here, found me. He asked what I was doing in there, but I didn't explain. He then asked if I was interested in taking photography, and I desperately needed a distraction, so I said yes. There was one other boy, his son, who was in the activity. He became my best friend," he straightened up in his seat and glanced at me, then looked away. "They moved away to Australia last year. The school hired a new teacher, got two other students to take the class, but it's not really the same. I miss them. But I never let go of this."

Taylor turned and stared at me. "You would like this place,"

"What makes you think that?" I asked.

He shrugged. "Like I said earlier, you're like me. You would love this. Not as much as I do …"

I laughed.

"But you will," he said. "Give it a shot?"

I smiled. "Why not?"

He smiled back, a smile that quickly faded, and then looked at the ground. "I know what you're thinking," he told me.

He does? I thought, but on the outside, I just blankly stared. "What do you mean?" I asked, trying to sound clueless.

"You're wondering if what they said was true," he said. "If I really am adopted."

He paused, waiting for me to admit it, that he was right, but I didn't. I didn't know how to.

So he went on. "No need to wonder anymore," he said. "No need to be cautious. I don't mind the question. I'm used to it. Technically, I really am adopted. But not exactly."

My mind was buzzing with this new information, but I couldn't process it correctly. I guess he thought I needed an explanation, so he gave me one.

"I wasn't ... abandoned at birth, and my mother didn't die or anything like that, but..." he gulped and didn't look away from the floor as if it was telling him something. "When I was eight years old, my father died and my mother decided that she didn't want me anymore. She gave me up. I was never put into the system, though. My grandparents took me in. Been living with them ever since."

I had no idea what to say. 'Sorry' just didn't seem right. Not for a tragedy like this. And what kind of person would give him up? Even though I didn't know him so well, I could tell that he was special. By the way he talked about things and actually cared about others. I wasn't about to ask him about his life before that, or what his parents were like because that would hurt him too much.

So we just sat there in silence that unbelievably wasn't awkward, but comfortable. There was no sound but our breathing, each of us just enjoying the company and lost in our own thoughts, but our thoughts were focused on each other.

After a while, he sighed. "Well," he said. "It's official."

"What is?"

He finally looked up at me and I got to see his beautiful brown eyes. "You're no longer a stranger."

"No, I guess I'm not," I agreed. "And neither are you."

He smiled. "Then what am I?"

"A friend," I replied. "And I think that with our screwed-up lives, we could both use one."

"We really could," he held out his hand. "Friends."

I shook it firmly and nodded. "Friends."

Taylor and I became closer and closer friends, and Rose liked him too. She thought he was the perfect addition to our small group of outcasts. He was like a brother to me, which was a good thing. I really needed friends at that time.

Because soon enough, my heart was shattered right when it had begun to mend itself.

My father died.

We all knew that it was inevitable, that it would've happened anyway, but it still took us by surprise. One morning, everything is okay. I get back from school, and it hits me like a ton of bricks. Right when my mom told me the news, I ran upstairs and locked myself in my bedroom, tuning out the sound of her screaming my name. I felt the strength go out of me and fell to my knees. I couldn't help but feel like it was all my fault. I hadn't tried enough, I hadn't talked to him enough, I hadn't done enough, I hadn't done this, I hadn't done that, and now I couldn't, I wished, but I couldn't. I didn't even go into bed. I just sat on the floor with my knees pulled up to my chest and my head in my hands, and I think that I cried, but I'm not sure, but I remember tissues, and I think I screamed, screamed at nothing, but I don't know, I just remember waking up the next morning with a sore throat.

I remember phone calls from Rose and Taylor, but I don't remember hearing their voices on the other line. I remember broken glass, but I don't remember what I broke. What I remember clearly is that I did not leave my room for an entire week after the funeral. After seeing my father's body, pale and stiff and lifeless, about to be six feet underground, after seeing the tombstone that read *Daniel Marshal Anne, Beloved Father and Husband,* I couldn't take it. I ran home and told everyone to wake me up when he came back. I didn't cat and barely slept, and when I did, I dreamt of old memories with him, so I guess I didn't want to sleep because I didn't want the flashbacks.

Every day, my mother would knock on the door, telling me I needed to get out and face it eventually. On the eighth day of keeping myself prisoner, I opened the door and asked her, "How are you not grieving? How are you not the same way I am?"

My mom looked at my messed up hair, tear-streaked face and bloodshot eyes. She looked at my body, noticed how thin I was. And then she opened her arms, and I gladly went into them, holding her tightly.

"Because," she whispered in my ear. "I know he wouldn't want us to be like this. I know that he would want us to move on and cope the best we can. It's going to be all right, sweetheart. But we have to accept it. There's no way to change it."

"I know there's not," I whispered back. "But it hurts."

"I know it does," she said. "We're going to be okay. He wouldn't want us to be like this."

I nodded and stayed in her hug a bit longer, and I felt this sort of relief in my chest. I had finally let him go, and I knew that it was for the best.

Five months later.

Taylor had told Rose and I a month earlier that he was moving in July. We spent that entire month together, never leaving each other's side. He was moving to Wisconsin, about nine hundred miles away from our humble home in Pennsylvania. I didn't want to lose him, and I knew that he felt that way too. But he had no choice. His grandparents wanted to move there, thinking it was the best thing to leave the place that bad memories still haunted.

"It's inevitable," he told us.

And I remember thinking *Death is inevitable. Bad and good things are inevitable. There are lots of things that are inevitable, but this isn't.*

But he was right. We begged and begged, but no matter what, he was still moving. And since he was only fourteen, he had no say in it.

On his last day in Philadelphia, we spent the entire day in his house, sitting in his empty bedroom, talking rarely and casting dark shadows and eerie echoes that bounced off the walls. Rose was with us until ten, but then she had to leave to be somewhere by lunchtime. We were left alone there.

"Do you remember when we first met?" he asked, breaking the silence.

I nodded. "You were in the darkroom."

He smiled. "And I first saw your face when you were squinting to try to see me."

I laughed. "My eyes had refused to adjust!"

"It was adorable," he leaned over and lightly poked my cheek. "The way your cheeks puffed up like that."

"Well, I was also crying," I said. "And I'm an ugly crier."

He tilted his head, thinking about it, and then said, "Yeah, you are."

I playfully shoved him. "You're mean!"

He shoved me back, laughing. "You said it first!"

"You weren't supposed to agree!"

"Well, that's what brothers do, isn't it?"

"Well, you're a *mean* brother!"

"Am not! I'm the way every brother is."

"I should disown you."

"You know what I think?"

"What?"

"That you'd be an *idiot* for disowning me."

"Then call me an idiot because you've been disowned!"

"No no no no no, I was kidding! Take me back!"

"Take you back?" I raised my eyebrows at him.

"AS YOUR BROTHER."

I laughed. "Fine, you're my brother again."

"Yay!" he said, and I gave him a look. "What?"

"Don't say 'yay'."

"Why?"

"It sounds weird."

"*Yay*!"

"*No*!"

We stayed like that until six, with me disowning him and taking him back so many times I'd lost count. His grandmother eventually came and said that it was time for him to leave. We both stood up, slowly, and then he hugged me for one last time. He finally let me go and headed to leave, but then turned to look at me.

"See you," he said, his voice breaking.

My eyes were burning, and I could feel myself choking up, but I actually laughed at that. He smiled at me, obviously wanting me to say it back.

"See you," I said.

And though I didn't realize it at the time, that was the moment I gave up on just about everything. I had lost my dad, a friend, and my brother in less than a year, so why would I believe that there was someone looking out for me?

CHAPTER TWELVE

I open my eyes, and I am in a hospital room with a tube in my arm pumping a clear liquid into my blood and a cannula to help me breathe. There is one nurse in the room, her back turned to me, folding a blanket on a chair. I slowly turn my head towards the window to see what time it is. It's dark outside, in the middle of the night.

The nurse finally turns to me, and her eyes widen when she sees that I'm awake.

"You woke up!" she exclaims happily.

Um …

"Could I have a cup of water?" I ask.

She nods eagerly and quickly pours me a cup from a glass pitcher. I'm too weak to move my arms, so she puts the cup to my lips, and I take small sips. She puts the cup on top of a small table and then rushes out of the room, probably to get the doctor, telling me she'll be right back.

I look around, taking in my surroundings.

Why am I here? I wonder.

I see balloons all over the place, some teddy bears, and on the table next to me that she put the cup on, I see a pile of cards.

I reach over to take them, which requires all the strength in me, and I put the pile on my stomach. I pick up the first one and open it. Inside is a long note scribbled, and I read it.

Marissa, it reads. *You've been in the hospital for three days now. Unconscious. I'm beginning to wonder if you'll ever be able to read any of the things I'm writing to you. You will. You have to. Anyway, in these notes is just a little bit of the things I want to say. I sit in your room every day, talking to you, or maybe I'm just talking to nothing, or myself ... I don't know, but they said that you might be able to hear or remember some of the things I said while you were asleep ... did you?*

I miss you, Marissa ... we all do. I've been sleeping here in the chair next to you, but today they told me not to, that I have to go home after my visit. I'll come back tomorrow, I promise, and I'll stay until you wake up.

Pinky promise,

Leon.

I read the date that it was written, and it says *January 3*.

Suddenly it all comes back to me like a tsunami of memories.

I almost died.

I had a heart attack.

I reread the card again and then put it down. I have to try to remember what he said to me while I was asleep.

And then I do.

Every day, he would come here and talk to me, just like he said he did. Every day, he sobbed in the chair and fell asleep. Every day, he would hold my hand in his and tell me how everyone was doing. He told me that Rose didn't go to school for the entire week and came to visit me as often as he did. He said that Graham stayed late at school doing a surprise project for me. He said that my mother has been here every day, and would often come to see how I was while he was still talking to me.

Every day, he would lift my hand a bit and lightly kiss it.

The nurse comes back in with the doctor following behind, and they smile.

"You're awake," the doctor says. He rushes over to the machines in the room, checking my heart rate and some other stuff I don't know.

They whisper about my condition and say some things to me, and I nod as if I understand, but I don't. I'm sixteen; I should not have had a heart attack. I should not be in a hospital room after being unconscious for three days. I should not be so concerned about my health.

I should not have been anorexic in the first place.

"How long have you been this way?" the doctor asks, bringing me back to reality.

I tilt my head in confusion. "What do you mean?"

"How long have you been starving yourself?" he repeats.

I feel my face burn, and I look away from his gaze. "I started over the summer after my eighth-grade year."

He nods and writes something down on the notepad he brought with him.

He whispers something more to the nurse and then heads out of the room. The nurse smiles at me and adjusts the blanket covering me to keep me warmer.

"Get some sleep," she says. "Some people are going to visit in the morning."

And even though I've already slept for three days, once the lights are out, so am I.

When I wake up in the morning, I look over to the chair next to my bed and see my mother sitting there.

"Good morning," she smiles weakly, trying to be casual, but I can see the pained expression in her eyes.

"Hi, Mom," I reply.

"Are you feeling better?" she asks, and I nod numbly. "Do you remember what happened? They said that your mind would be a little fuzzy after everything that went on."

I nod again. "Yes, I remember." I pause, and even though I'm pretty sure I already know the answer, I ask, "What day is it?"

"January fourth," she says. "Happy New Year."

"I slept right through New Year's?" I say.

She nods. "Yep. Your friends were all here at midnight."

"They shouldn't have been," I say. "They should've been out having fun somewhere."

"They wanted to make sure you were okay."

I search her tired eyes. "How's Rose?"

"She's fine," says Mom. "She's waiting outside for her turn to come in and visit you."

She stares at me and holds her gaze for so long that it makes me uncomfortable, and I look away.

"How long?" she asks me, and unlike the way I replied to the doctor last night, I don't need an explanation.

"Since the summer before high school," I say.

I see tears well up in her eyes, but she tries to hold them back. "Why didn't you tell me?"

I told whoever bothered to ask. The answer is right on the tip of my tongue, but I don't say it, afraid of hurting her more than I already have. So instead, I give her the second reason.

"Because I knew what you would say," I tell her. "And I didn't want you to worry."

She clears her throat. "Why did you do it?"

I stare up at the ceiling, holding back my tears as much as she is, but my voice breaks anyway. "When I was in the eighth grade, I was a little bit overweight. By about ten—fifteen—pounds,"

She nods, remembering.

"I wanted to lose some weight, so I started eating just some fruits and salad, and in a week I lost seven pounds," I said. "People complimented me, said I looked great. I liked the feeling. So I thought, 'What if I lose ten more pounds?' and it seemed like a great idea at the time, but once I did it, people started giving me weird looks and whispering around me. I thought that I had gained more weight and tried to lose some more. Then people said I was too skinny, and I gained some more but then felt disgusting and wanted to lose it again."

I can't bear to look at my mother's reaction, so I glance around the room, looking anywhere except at her. "It stayed in that pattern for a while. And even though I soon came to the conclusion that I was anorexic, I didn't stop. I couldn't," I scoff. "We see where that got me now."

I finally look at her, and I see silent tears spill over onto her cheeks.

"I'm sorry," she whispers, staring at the floor.

"For what?" I ask.

"For not being there enough," she says. "I never … I never knew what was going on in your life. I never knew about any of this." She takes a deep breath. "I need to quit my job."

"What?" I say, fully awake now. "No! Mom, you love this job. You can't quit!"

"What else can I do?" she asks, still not quite meeting my eyes

"Just …" I think for another solution. "Don't work *as much.* But don't quit altogether. You love working here, and you're good at it."

She thinks it over and then smiles a bit. "How about this: from now on, I'll work only until four in the afternoon, and I don't work on weekends or holidays at all."

I smile. "I'd like that."

And then I remember something. "I thought that only family was allowed to stay, or even visit."

She grins slyly. "We may or may not have said that Leon's your cousin. And that Rose is your sister."

I laugh. "Nice move, Mom."

"I know. You have some really great friends out there."

"Yeah, I know."

"Two of them stayed here all night."

"I really thought that wasn't allowed."

"It's not. They stayed in the waiting room, snuck in, fell asleep, and the nurses kept having to wake them up in the middle of the night to go home."

"Oh. Was it Rose and Leon?"

"Yeah," my mom looks down. "He reminds me of someone," she says.

"Oh?" I say though I realize a second later who she's talking about.

She looks up into my hazel eyes. "I think you already know who."

I do.

Leon reminds her of a younger version of my father.

She glances at the clock and then stands up. "My time is up in here. Rose is waiting outside. I'll send her in." She comes over and gives me a hug. "Be nice."

"I'll do my best."

She releases me and heads for the exit, stopping to blow me a kiss and then closes the door. I am left by myself in complete silence, thinking about everything that's happened to me over just a week.

My thoughts are interrupted two minutes later when Rose opens the door and stumbles inside. She freezes when she sees me, and the door closes behind her. Her blue eyes are red and have these dark circles around them, and her usually combed and beautiful blonde hair is a mess. She is thin, and her arms hang at her sides.

"Oh my gosh," she chokes out and falls to her knees next to the hospital bed.

"Rose," I say, reaching out for her hand, but my arm doesn't reach that far. "Rose, it's okay. I'm okay."

"I'm sorry," she mumbles in between sobs, her voice muffled by the blanket. "I'm so, so sorry."

Why is everyone apologizing?

"Rose, there's nothing you need to apologize for," I say.

She pops her head up. "How can you say that?" she demands. "I knew! I knew about all of this! I knew that you weren't eating, but I didn't do anything about it, I didn't tell *anyone!* I thought that you were getting better these past months ..." her voice trails off and she begins to cry again, quietly this time. "I'm sorry."

"It's not your fault," I tell her. "I told you not to tell anyone. And I—I tricked you into believing that I was getting better."

She inhales, trying to stop crying. "W-what?"

I sigh. "I pretended to eat in front of you, but I threw the food away. I didn't want you to worry about me."

She blinks.

"I should've told you the truth," I say. "And right now, you have every right to be mad at me."

She shakes her head quickly. "No. I can't be mad at you right now. In any other situation, I would've been since you lied to me, but right now, I can't be. Not when this has happened."

She pulls herself to her feet and sits down next to me on the bed. "You should've told me," she says.

"I know," I agree. "I should've trusted you. And I don't know why I told you to keep it a secret. That was stupid of me."

"I still blame myself for not telling anyone, though," Rose admits.

I open my arms and hug her, and thankfully, she hugs me back.

"I've missed you," she says into my shoulder.

"I've missed you too," I reply and then release her. "Now honestly, I don't feel like talking about this while I'm stuck here. Could we talk about something else?"

She giggles, and it's nice to hear her laugh again. "Sure," she says. "What do you want to talk about?"

"How about ..." I pause. "You and Graham?"

She rolls her eyes. "What about me and Graham?"

"Don't act so innocent," I say. "I've noticed the way you guys are around each other."

"Oh?" she says. "And how exactly are we? A bit like you and Leon?"

"Exactly," I reply, without realizing what I'm saying. It's only when her eyes widen and her smile brightens that I realize what I just said.

"Wait, hold on—" I begin, but it's too late.

"Yes!" she exclaims, pumping her fist into the air. "I knew it! When were you going to tell me?"

"Whoa, tell you what?" I ask.

"That you two are going out."

"We're just friends."

"Yeah, right. He likes you *a lot.*"

"How would you know?"

Rose rolls her eyes. "You're so oblivious."

"What did I do?"

"Can you not see the signs?" she exclaims.

"What signs?" I ask. "*Friends.* Nothing more, nothing less."

"He talks about you all the time."

"In a friendship way."

"He always wants to be with you."

"Because friends hang out."

"And he told me he likes you."

"As in—*whoa.*"

"Yep," she smiles triumphantly. "Told me that straight up this week."

"Just like that?"

"Just like that."

"How, exactly?"

"We were hanging out," she explains. "Me, him, and Graham. We were talking about you, of course, wallowing …"

"Wallowing?" I repeat.

"Yeah," she says. "You know, being upset, crying, feeling bad, eating ice cream except we couldn't even eat. *Wallowing.*"

"Should I question it?"

"No."

"Okay, continue."

"Anyway, all of a sudden he just said, 'Man, I hope she's okay. I really like her.'"

"That doesn't mean anything …"

"I'm not done," she cuts me off. "So Graham and I asked, 'Wait, you like her as in …' and he was like, 'Yeah, I thought you knew.'"

"*Oh, my gosh.*"

"He said that he told you, though."

Then I remember what he said at Graham's house on Christmas.

"Look, I understand if this is weird for you. It's weird for me too. I didn't think that I would ever fall in love so easily. I didn't think that it would be with you either."

I look back at Rose now. "Yeah," I say. "He did."

She throws her hands up, exasperated. "Then why are you so surprised?"

"I dunno," I shrug. "I guess I just didn't think he meant it."

"He *does,*" she says. "And I don't mean to be pushy right now, especially since you literally just woke up, but there's this guy out there who really likes you. Don't miss your chance."

I sigh and look up at the ceiling. "I hate you right now."

"Nah," she shakes her head. "You always love me. Now, it's time for someone else to visit you."

"Graham?"

"He's working on something at the school," she says. "Couldn't come. So I'm guessing you know who's next."

I roll my eyes as she heads for the door and then think of something.

"Wait a minute!" I call, stopping her. "You never answered my question about you and Graham."

She smiles suspiciously. "I've gotten better at stalling."

"Rose—"

"Bye!" she steps out of the room and closes the door.

I let out a groan of frustration and stare at the ceiling, listening to the voices outside the walls. They're too quiet to understand, but I could tell that it's a conversation between Rose and Leon.

"Man up!" she raises her voice, and I hear my mother laugh and catch a glimpse of her face through the window. They seem better than they did when they came in to visit. It makes me feel better.

Someone takes a step back, and then for a split second I see Leon's face, but I can't see whether he's smiling or what he's thinking. He steps away, and then I can't see them anymore. Rose lowers her voice until all I hear are sounds like the muffled voice on the other end of a phone as they block the receiver.

And then there's a knock on the door.

I see the knob twist, and it slowly creaks open.

A head of light-brown floppy hair peeks in, and I smile.

"Hey, Graeme."

He smiles back, walks in, closes the door but stays leaning against it, blocking the window. He pulls his sweater tighter around himself and puts his hands in the pockets of his jeans. "Been a while, hasn't it, Miss Anne?"

"Three days," I correct him.

"Which is a while."

"For you."

"Maybe."

I chuckle, and he smiles, but there's something about it that's forced. And then when I cough, for a second there's a flicker of worry on his face. He's still worried about me. He's not supposed to be.

He can't be.

I can't help but ask him, "Did you miss me?"

I say it in a joking way, but I'm really not joking, and I just said it like that to lighten the mood a bit.

He scoffs and says sarcastically, "Me? Nah. Didn't even notice you were gone."

Now I force a smile, but there's a certain tension in the air between us, and I don't know why.

"On the other hand," he says, walking over and sitting next to me on the hospital bed. He reaches for my cold hand and holds it in his warm one. I suddenly feel all tingly inside. "It's not very nice to leave a guy all alone after he put so much thought into a date for the girl he has a crush on."

"Next time, I'll try not to leave early," I reply trying to be cool when I'm freaking out inside.

"So there's going to be a next time?" he asks, raising one eyebrow.

"Could be," I say, blushing and hoping he doesn't notice.

He gives a half-smile, which quickly fades. "Now, I'm going to stop stalling and talk about what I'm really thinking about."

I get nervous, and my heart begins to beat faster. I calm down, reminding myself that I ended up here because of a heart attack and now is not the time to have another.

"Why?" he asks.

"Why, what?"

"Why'd you do it?" he says. "Stop eating. Starving yourself like that. More importantly is the question I'm asking myself every day."

"What?"

"Why I didn't say anything about it," he says, his eyes unfocused, looking at me but not really. Zoned-out, remembering or just thinking about something. I see tears well up in his eyes. "I was so stupid."

"You said lots of things to me," I reassure him. "I was just too stubborn to listen, too blind to see what I was doing to myself."

"But I didn't say anything to anyone else," he replies, coming back to reality. "If I did, even if I had lost your friendship, at least you would've been better. You wouldn't have almost died like you did. And I can't help but feel like it's all my fault."

Now, where does that sound familiar?

There's a look of guilt in his glassy eyes and a look of pity mixed in there too. I feel a twinge of anger towards him for feeling bad for me, but I know that I would pity him also if he were in my place.

"It's not," I say firmly. "Leon, I brought this on myself. I didn't think of the consequences. Just of my actions."

He takes my hand again. "Isn't that hard? I mean, not to eat every day?"

"In the beginning, yeah," I admit. "But after a little bit, I got used to it. And the hunger turned into this buzzing numbness in the back of my mind. It was this kind of—horribly—addictive thing, I guess. You kind of get addicted to the idea of knowing that you're skinny, and skinny is pretty in our world."

"Our world is *stupid*," he says, practically spitting the words out. "Our society is stupid. If this is what they do to people like you."

On the first week we met, that's something he said to me. He cursed our society for all the things it does, and then I reminded him that he really was a part of society. I wonder if he remembers that too.

"People like me?"

"People who really, truly are amazing in every way possible," he explains. "And then they suddenly stop believing that they are."

I feel my face turning red at the compliment, and the butterflies come back. And then when my face continues burning, I realize that I am almost crying. Again.

That's too many tears in one morning.

"I never believed I was in the first place," I answer honestly, trying my best to keep my voice from cracking. "I've always thought that I was just put here to fill up a space. But once I started to get older, I decided that maybe I could fill the space up more by being better."

"Better at what?" he asks, the question sounding a bit more like an accusation.

"Not really better," I correct myself. "Just... good enough, I guess. Pretty enough. Tall enough," I exhale, and mutter, "Skinny enough."

He looks at me, not with pity, but with concern, which I'd prefer. He reaches over and gently wipes away the tears in my eyes.

"You're right about one thing," he says. "You're not good enough. Never were."

He leans closer until he's only a few inches away from my face. "You are so. Much. More."

He leans even closer and kisses my forehead, and we stay like that, with his lips still there. And he mutters, "There was never anything wrong with you. I promise you that. God put you here for a reason, and that reason is not to be questioning your existence. *You are not here to fill up a space*. You are beautiful, valued, wanted. You have to believe that you are special to God ..." And then he pulls away, and looks at me for a while; staring at me, and I can't look away. "You're special to me."

He gives my hand a squeeze and then stands up and heads for the door, only to stop right in front of it and turn to me.

"So," he says. "You did it because the world told you that you weren't good enough? That you have to be skinny and wear makeup and wear nice clothes to be pretty?"

I nod, suddenly very much aware of my messed up hair and the cannula. "Pretty much."

He chuckles. "Well, you look very beautiful in that hospital gown."

And then he opens the door, and he's gone.

CHAPTER THIRTEEN

"We need to do something to cheer you up," Rose announces as we walk out of the hospital.

It's a Sunday since school has already started up again. I'm not behind, thankfully, because they always brought me my work after school and helped me do it, mostly by giving me the answers or helping me Google them.

It's February eight and it's cold, but it's not snowing. Just gray skies and frozen sidewalks and snow from last week's storm. I'm suddenly grateful for the black hoodie and leggings they brought me. As for the shirt, I just have a grayish long sleeve one that's a bit big on me, like it's always been.

"I am cheered up!" I argue. "I just got out of the hospital and got rid of that stupid hospital gown."

"It didn't look bad," Leon says.

"Yes, it did. It was huge and thick and fluffy."

"Fluffy?"

"Fluffy. I hated it."

"Well, I still don't think it looked bad."

I glare at him, but he doesn't stop.

"It didn't!" he says. "Not on you, anyway."

I drop my gaze. "I'm still glad I got rid of it," I shoot back, but I'm blushing.

"I don't blame you for that, though." He smiles. "Getting rid of it means you got out."

"After over a month."

"You still got out, didn't you?"

"Guys," Graham interrupts. "Stop flirting. Rose wasn't finished."

"Keep defending your girlfriend, Graham, you're pretty good at it," I say.

"Shut up."

"We're not dating!" Rose cuts in.

"Yet," I say.

At that, Graham blushes and looks down.

"Exactly," I grin.

"Anyway!" Rose says, saving Graham. "We need to celebrate the fact that you're better."

"I'm not completely better."

"You're eating."

"I can't eat so much. The doctors said that my body isn't used to it so I would end up throwing it up."

"You're still eating."

"I also have to take pills."

"IT'S AN IMPROVEMENT."

I put my hands up in surrender. "Okay, okay. We're the only people who wouldn't take something like this so seriously."

Leon's face softens, and he looks at me. "We *do* take it seriously. We just …"

I tilt my head. "Just what?"

"We know that you don't like it when everything is so serious and gloomy. You feel awkward in it. So, we're acting like nothing happened for you."

I smile. "It's better that way. And I especially appreciate the fact that you know I feel very awkward in gloominess."

He smiles back. "Of course."

"You're still flirting!" Graham jumps in.

Rose pretends to gag.

I roll my eyes.

"Oh, leave us alone," I say to them. "So, Rose. What do you plan on us doing?"

"First," she smiles eagerly and her eyes light up. "A makeover."

We all groan.

She puts her hands on her hips. "Come on, guys! And not for you, just for Marissa."

The boys high-five, and I groan.

"Fine, not a full-out makeover," she says. "Just a haircut and painting your nails."

"That sounds like a full-out makeover," I say.

"No, that would include makeup and new outfits."

"I'm good. That would take too long."

"Then, a haircut?"

"Fine."

"Yes!" she squeals. "Let's go."

She pulls my hand and drags me out to the parking lot to Leon's truck.

"Why do we always take his car?" Graham complains. "I have a car too, you know!"

"Is your car here?" Rose asks him.

"No."

"That's why."

I look over my shoulder at Leon, and he smiles at me.

Help me! I mouth silently.

He puts his hands up and shrugs as if to say, *It's out of my hands.*

I roll my eyes, but he's probably right.

When it's up to Rose, there's nothing you can do.

We pile into the car, Rose shoving me in the front seat so I can be next to Leon and, my own theory, so she can be next to Graham.

Leon starts the car, backs up out of the parking lot, and we take off.

"Where to?" Leon asks Rose once we're on the road.

"Guess."

"The mall?"

"Where else?"

He heads in the direction of our local mall, and halfway there, much to my surprise, he reaches for my hand.

Even more to my surprise, I let him hold it.

Rose and Graham don't seem to notice, especially since it's hidden, thanks to our seats.

Leon sighs and when I glance over at him to sneak a glimpse of his face, he seems relieved. Happy.

I wonder if my cheeks are as red as I think they are.

I feel this weird spark inside me, and I don't know what it is, but I like the feeling of it. I realize it must be the butterflies again. Or the zoo.

We pull into the parking lot, and after giving my hand one last squeeze, he lets go, only because we both know he has to.

He takes out the keys, and we step out of the car, slamming the doors shut behind us.

"Last time we were here, we ran through the entire parking lot," Leon remembers.

I shake my head. "No."

They don't need an explanation. The doctors also said that I'm too weak to do any exercise besides walking. And I have a limited time for even that.

So we walk together towards the doors, Rose and Graham ahead of us, Leon and I trailing closely behind.

"Are you really up to this?" he asks me quietly.

I nod. "Yeah."

"You literally just got out."

"They said I'm free to go," I point out. "And I'm not going to be walking so much. We're just going to whatever salon Rose likes so she can do what she wants with me, and that's it. Then I'll go home and rest, as if I haven't been doing that for the past month."

"It hasn't been that long. It's only February."

"But it's *still* February," I say. "And I've wasted that much time in a hospital staring at the same ceiling, eating the same horrid food, and taking the same medication, which I *still* have to take. All because I thought I wasn't good enough and chose not to eat about three years ago. I'm not making that mistake again. I'm not wasting any more time."

Leon purses his lips and nods. "I don't want to waste any more time either. But it's not really my choice."

He doesn't think I know that he's not talking about the same thing anymore. But really, it's obvious, and I honestly agree with him. I don't want to waste any more time. But it's not as easy as they make it seem in movies. It's not so easy to trust someone after you've been let down your whole life, whether it was someone who betrayed you, someone who gave in to addiction and, soon enough, death, someone who was whisked away from you, but not by choice, or maybe just someone who wasn't there for you as much as they should've been.

I've been let down one too many times.

And even though I know that it's inevitable to be let down again, I'd prefer to avoid it as much as I possibly can.

But I can't avoid this.

I can't avoid him.

We enter the doors, and I turn to Rose.

"So, where exactly are you going to take me?" I ask her.

"Where do I always go?" she asks.

I think for a second. "The place across from *Comix*."

"What's *Comix*?" Graham asks.

"Her favorite comic book store," Leon tells him.

"How do you know that?"

"I took her there once."

"We're going there?" I ask Rose.

"Yup," she says. "It's the best place."

"Then let's go," I say, and then we all head towards the escalators to get to the first floor.

"Am I the only one who doesn't know where this place is?" Graham asks, struggling to keep up.

"Well, yeah," I say.

"I mean, Rose goes there for … whatever she does," Leon says, receiving a glare from my blonde-haired best friend. "And Marissa and I go to *Comix* together. I'm surprised you haven't been there."

"Yeah, since you're such a nerd when it comes to Star Wars and Superman—"

"No," Graham cuts me off as we step off the escalator and continue walking. "No, the Superman comics are overrated. I mean, sure, they're good, but really, it's not as great as it seems."

"I've never read it," I say. "Especially not after watching the newest movie."

"Gosh, that movie was horrible," Rose says.

"I know!" Graham agrees. "Every time you thought it ended, BAM, another plot twist to screw your life up. It was the never-ending movie."

"They ran out of ideas after his dad got sucked into a tornado," Leon says.

"That was the only good scene," I agree.

Rose leans over and whispers in my ear, "Yeah, and it didn't hurt that Clark Kent wasn't bad-looking when he was younger."

I laugh at that, and Leon looks at us. "Do I want to know?"

"Not really."

"Now I really want to know."

"You're not going to," Rose says. "We're here."

I look up at the salon called, of all things, *Belle*, just like any other hair salon.

"Come on," Rose waves the guys inside but grabs a hold of my wrist to drag me in.

"Yeah, we're good," Graham says.

"We'll be at *Comix*!" Leon calls after us, and then they disappear in the store next door.

Rose goes to the front desk. "Hey, Greg."

He looks up and grins. "Rose! What can we do for you today?"

"Actually, it's for my friend today," she explains. "Just a haircut and manicure."

"No pedicure?"

"Nope, not today."

"Which first?"

"Whichever one you can get first."

He looks over his shoulder at the manicure station and then turns back to us. "Lacy could take you right now."

"Great," she says. "How much?"

"Supposed to be about thirty, but I'll give you a discount and make the package twenty dollars."

Rose digs in her wallet and pulls out a crumpled twenty-dollar bill. "Thanks, Greg."

"No problem."

We head over to where a woman, Lacy I assume, is sitting, arranging her nail polish.

"Sit," she instructs, and I obey. "What color?"

"Um …" I look over all the colors. There's so many.

"Make it the stars," Rose jumps in. "And the moon."

Lacy nods. "You got it."

She does this whole process of cleaning my nails and removing the cuticles and dipping my fingers in water, I have no idea what for. She then puts a clear coat on each of my nails, then grabs this dark blue color and applies it. She grabs this tiny white nail polish with a thin brush and then does small designs of stars on them, and then on my ring finger, she does a pale half-moon. She adds another clear coat, gets this misty spray, which she puts all over my nails, and then nods.

"Done," she says, putting the things away. "Don't touch anything with your nails, okay?"

"Okay," I say. "Thank you."

"No problem."

Once I stand up, and Rose and I head to some seats to wait for my turn to cut my hair, I turn to her. "Peter Pan style?"

She smiles. "Second star to the right. I know how you love that stuff. You like it?"

I nod. "It looks cool. I should do this more often."

"I never thought I'd hear you say that."

"Neither did I."

"Marissa?" We look up to see the guy from the front desk, Greg, standing behind a faucet and a chair. "Your turn."

We stand up and head over to him. Rose stands next to him as I sit down in the chair and lean my head back.

"How do you want it?" he asks, turning on the faucet and beginning to wash my long hair.

"Cut it," Rose says. "Make it short. With layers."

"How short?"

"A little bit above the shoulder," I tell him. I can sense Rose smiling.

"Highlights?" Greg asks.

"Yeah, to replace the old ones," I say.

"Same blonde color, on the tips and bangs," Rose says.

"Got it," he says. He finishes washing my hair and then drapes a little towel over my shoulders so it doesn't get my shirt wet.

He leads me to one of the tall salon chairs, which I sit down in, and he begins to brush my hair. He ties it in a ponytail at the correct length and then pulls out some scissors and cuts it off. It suddenly feels lighter.

He trims it after that, puts some highlights, dries it, and before I know it, he steps back and announces, “Done!”

I look in the mirror and smile. It’s very short, which will make it easier so I won’t have to constantly tie it when I’m skateboarding. The blonde bits are brighter than the old ones which had gone dull, and even after I run my fingers through it, shake my head, scruff it up, it still looks good. My bangs are even more in my face, but I like it like that. I always have.

I can’t remember the last time I liked what I saw when I looked in the mirror.

I jump up from my chair, thank Greg, and then head over to Rose, who was in the waiting room reading a magazine.

“So?” I ask her, and she looks up and grins. “What do you think?”

She stands up. “You look *amazing*!” she says. “Seriously, this looks way better than how your hair used to be. We should’ve done this sooner. You’ve always had your hair long.”

"Not anymore," I smile. "Come on, let's go find Graham and Leon."

"Okay."

We walk out, and before we can walk into *Comix*, they walk out, each holding a plastic bag with comic books in them.

"You owe me five bucks," Leon says.

"Yeah, yeah," Graham reaches into his wallet and hands him a five-dollar bill, then turns to Rose. "We made a bet. I said that you'd be out in half an hour, he said an hour and a half."

"We took that long?" Rose asks.

"Yup," Leon says, taking the money from Graham.

"Where's Marissa?" Graham asks.

Rose and I laugh, and he smiles. "Nah, I'm joking, but you really do look different," he says. "I'm not *that* stupid."

"Really?" I ask.

"Shut up."

I give him a sarcastic smile, and he shoots one back at me.

Rose claps her hands together. "Well," she says. "I say that we should go get some ice cream."

"How about frozen yogurt?" Graham suggests.

I hesitate at first. It's the frozen yogurt shop with the parking lot, but it's also the one I used to go to with James. I mean, I like going to the parking lot with my friends but going inside brings me memories. I look over at Rose, and she knows what I'm thinking.

"Sometimes," she says. "You have to make good memories to pile over the bad ones."

I turn back to Graham. "What're we waiting for?"

Leon drops me off at home after we eat (I could only have small amounts), but I don't stay there. Once they are out of sight, I grab the keys to my mom's car, scribble her a note saying that I am still with my friends and will be back later, and then head out.

I know how to drive. My mom taught me last year, but I don't have a license or even a permit yet. So if I get caught, I'm in trouble.

At first, I have no idea where I'm going. But then, I decide to go back to the place I just came from.

The Frozen Yogurt shop.

When we left, the place was closing, so I know that it's empty right now, which is what I'm looking for. All I need is to be alone right now. At least for a little while.

I pull into the parking lot, putting the car right in the middle of the lanes, not bothering to park it correctly, not wanting to. I take the keys out of the ignition, open the door, and step out.

It's not late. Only about six. But since it's winter, the sunset was about an hour ago and it's dark out. It's peaceful.

Most people are afraid of the dark. Afraid of what's lurking in it and the unsettling mood of it. I don't fear it. In fact, I find comfort in it. I never knew why. I guess it's because of the very fact that most people fear it. Because you don't know what's in it. You can't see what's beyond the limited light you make for yourself. So in a crowded place that's dark, you could imagine that you're alone if you can't see them. I love that.

I kneel down on the ground and then lean back until I'm lying down in an odd position, with my feet touching my rib cages. Then I stretch my legs out in front of me and just stay there, staring at the sky, at all the stars in it, and I imagine that they're shining for me, that they came out tonight because I did too.

I remember that Leon once said that no one could hear you out here. There's no one around, but should I risk it? Yes, I should.

I sit up, kneeling again, and then I put my head between my hands and scream. I scream, letting out all the frustration and anger and sadness that's been building up inside me for three years. I scream, not caring who hears me anymore. I let out everything. All of my depressing thoughts, all of the things inside me that said I wasn't good enough. I scream until my throat hurts, and then I stop, catching my breath.

I stay like that, crouched over, and I feel tears in my eyes.

I'm done.

"That must be some beast inside you if you want to get it out so desperately."

I don't look up. I know who it is. "What are you doing here?"

"I tried calling you," Leon says. "Your mom picked up. She asked if you were with me. That was when I figured out that you didn't go home, but came to the first place you could think of. Where you could be alone. So I told her yes, that you were with me because I didn't want her to worry. And so I could come here myself."

I'm still catching my breath, panting. "You didn't have to. I'm fine."

"I know, but I *wanted* to come here," he says. "I could tell. You weren't as okay as you said you were, as you say you are now. You just said you were so none of us would be worried."

"I'm surprised that you noticed and Rose didn't."

"Oh no, she noticed. She asked me what was up with you. I told her that I don't know. She was going to ask you, but I told her not to. And she knows that I'm here right now, but didn't come. She thought that I could cheer you up more than she could."

"What made her think that?"

"Well, we both know a lot about you. She was the one who knew you'd be here; I was the one who knew why. That says enough about the different ways we understand you."

I sigh. "I just can't."

I hear his shuffling feet as he steps closer to me. He kneels down in front of me.

"You can't what?" he asks.

"I can't pretend anymore," I say. "I've been pretending to be okay for so long. And there were times where I could actually believe I was. I'm not. I accept that now. I'm a screwed up, horrible mess …"

"But hey," Leon cuts me off. He reaches for my hands and pulls them away from my head. I still don't look at him, though. "Aren't we all?"

"I'm worse than most,"

"No no no no no," he says, grabbing my wrists and holding them. "Don't say that. Don't ever say that, don't even think that. Marissa. Marissa, look at me," I finally look at him. "Listen to me: you are *human.* Jesus didn't die for some alien race, it was for us, and we are sinners, all of us. You have to believe it."

"I want to believe it," I cut him off.

"Listen," he continues, "humans are like that. We criticize ourselves. We—we don't like anything that we do, so we hurt ourselves as a punishment when we screw something up, whether it's emotionally," he gestures to me, "or physically. It's the way we are. If we do something wrong, something we regret deeply, we don't pat ourselves on the back and say, 'Well, I tried, didn't I?' No, we give up and beat ourselves up about it. It's not right. And we don't even know why we do this. We understand ourselves no more than the other animals living in our world or the monsters living under our beds."

He takes a breath, looking into my eyes, and I think I see tears in his own. "You are not worse than anyone," he whispers. "I won't say that you're perfect because you're not. But you're imperfect in every way, but yet that's better than perfect. You're not a mess, and if you are, you're a beautiful mess because everyone who's human is. Though you look better than others. You can thank God for that one."

I laugh at that.

He sighs. "You know that saying, 'If you're not okay, then it's not the end'?"

I nod.

"That saying isn't true," he says. "There are so many people who die without being okay. They could die in a war, from a disease; in a car accident right after they got into a fight with someone they love, they could die from a bullet. We can't control how we die. But what we can control is how we spend the time while we're alive."

"Happily ever after isn't real, basically, is what you're saying," I say.

He pauses, thinking it over. "Yeah, basically, at least not in this world," he agrees. "I know that friends will fade, that there will be so many times that you fall in love and will break your heart. I know that; I know all of that. Life is not easy. But I also know that we have to appreciate the things we have before they slip right through our fingers and they're gone."

Nothing's ever really gone, though. The memories will always be there, you will always remember unless one day you wake up without a clue of what happened the day before, and you have amnesia. And even then if someone ever really meant something to you, then all you have to do is look at them, and you feel something inside you that you can't explain.

"According to the way life usually plays out," he continues, "this is the happiest ending we're going to get here. Because in the end, we'll both graduate from high school and go to different colleges. We'll grow up and possibly forget each other. That's just the way it works."

"I don't want that to happen."

"Neither do I, but what can we do?"

I shrug and make a face as if to say, *I got nothing.*

"I know I met you for a reason. That God let me meet you that day in the hallway for something," he continues. "And I guess someday, if you become just a memory, I'll look back on this and finally realize what it is."

He looks at me, sighs, and pulls me into a hug, wrapping his arms around my waist, and I wrap mine around his neck. "Just hold on a little while longer. It'll all be over soon."

I don't need to ask what he means. In some ways, I know. In others, I don't. I know that he means the pills and medication will be over soon. I know that he means the doctors will soon stop having to check on me. I know that he means I'll get through tomorrow without so many people staring at me and whispering. I know that he means he'll help me through all of that. But I know that he means something more. That's the part I don't know. What more he means. A part of me understands it, but I can't put it into words, no matter how hard I try.

And that's when I realize that though there may be no such thing as happily ever after, there is such a thing as true love. I've seen it before, with the way my mother looked at my father, even when he was on his deathbed. You can fall in love a thousand times, but only one time will it ever be true love. Some of them will leave a scar, but they will heal, not with Band-Aids or chocolate, but only with letting go. But those that leave a scar, you cannot simply stop loving them. A part of you will always care. But if you want to stop loving them, then that's how you know that you don't care as much as you used to.

There's also a different type of love that I've felt before. The way that Leon believes in a celestial being in heaven who loves everyone unconditionally, who gives us an infinite amount of chances, who gives us the power of free will and choice. I don't know how it's even possible to have that much love for so many horrible people in this horrible world, but Leon believes it.

And now, I believe it too.

I pull back, and we lean against each other, our foreheads touching. I reach for his right hand with my own and interlock my pinky with his.

"I promise," I say to him. "That I will not forget you. I will not forget how you helped me forget about everything going on. I will not forget all the times you cheered me up. I will not forget about any of this."

He lets out a shaky breath. "Promise me one more thing,"

"What is it?"

"Promise me you won't grow up."

I smile to myself. "Never."

"Pinky promise?"

I nod numbly. "Pinky promise."

He stands up and offers me a hand to help me up, which I take. I'm so short compared to him. The top of my head is level with his eyes, so he has to look down at me.

"One more question," he says, giving me a small smile.

"What is it?"

"How much do you trust me?" he asks, grinning now.

I hesitate for only a moment before telling him, "One hundred."

He smiles even bigger if that's possible.

"Well, in that case, there are two things I must ask of you."

"Which would be ...?"

"One, will you go to church with me?"

I laugh. "Seriously?"

"Seriously."

"Okay. Deal. What's next?"

"Well, you said you would tell me why you stopped trusting people once you trusted me completely," he reminds me.

"You and your good memory."

"Isn't it a good thing?"

"Depends,"

He laughs. "Well, are you going to tell me?"

I change the subject. "How'd you get here?"

"I walked."

"You need a ride home?"

He shrugs. "Sure."

As we head home that night, I look over at him singing along to a Coldplay song on the radio and wonder if it's even possible to forget someone like him, someone who taught me to live and love again. How could I forget someone who changed my life as much as he did?

Impossible.

www.ingramcontent.com/pod-product-compliance
Lightning Source LLC
Chambersburg PA
CBHW070905180626
46817CB00003B/924

9780692471432